Heather Park

Regency Romance

De-ann Black

Paperback edition published 2021

Heather Park

ISBN: 9798736398027

Also by De-ann Black (Romance, Action/Thrillers & Children's books). See her Amazon Author page or website for further details about her books, screenplays, illustrations, art and fabric designs.
www.De-annBlack.com

Romance:
The Tea Shop by the Sea
The Bookshop by the Seaside
The Sewing Bee
The Quilting Bee
Snow Bells Wedding
Snow Bells Christmas
Summer Sewing Bee
The Chocolatier's Cottage
Christmas Cake Chateau
The Beemaster's Cottage
The Sewing Bee By The Sea
The Flower Hunter's Cottage
The Christmas Knitting Bee
The Sewing Bee & Afternoon Tea
The Vintage Sewing & Knitting Bee
Shed In The City
The Bakery By The Seaside
Champagne Chic Lemonade Money
The Christmas Chocolatier
The Christmas Tea Shop & Bakery
The Vintage Tea Dress Shop In Summer
Oops! I'm The Paparazzi
The Bitch-Proof Suit

Action/Thrillers: Love Him Forever. Someone Worse. Electric Shadows. The Strife Of Riley. Shadows Of Murder.

Children's books: Faeriefied. Secondhand Spooks. Poison-Wynd. Wormhole Wynd. Science Fashion. School For Aliens.

Colouring books:
Summer Garden. Spring Garden. Autumn Garden. Sea Dream. Festive Christmas. Christmas Garden. Flower Bee. Wild Garden. Faerie Garden Spring. Flower Hunter. Stargazer Space. Bee Garden.

Contents

CHAPTER ONE

The excitement of the summer began with an unexpected invitation.

The letter arrived while the Ashby family were having breakfast. Tea, fresh baked bread, apple cake, spiced buns, butter, raspberry jam, and an array of other tasty treats were being tucked into at the dining table. The room was filled with chatter and the glow of morning sunlight.

'A letter arrived, ma'am.' Tilsy, a cheerful woman, happy to have been part of the Heathfield household staff for many years, handed the letter to the effervescent Mrs. Ashby.

Although, as head of the family, it should've been given to Mr. Ashby, the maid knew he would defer the handling of it to his wife while he read his newspaper and ate breakfast. He was accustomed to the chatter flitting around him, buzzing in the background, and sorely missed it on the rare occasions when the women of the household were all away visiting friends and relatives. His wife and three daughters — Evelyn, twenty–one, Annabel, nineteen, and Primrose, seventeen, were his joy.

Mrs. Ashby opened the letter, and her face lit up with delight as she made the announcement. 'We've all been invited to attend a ball at Heather Park.'

Sunlight streaming through the windows was no match for the warmth of excitement that sparked around the breakfast table.

Details of the date and time were quickly established. They'd been given very little notice, but this did not dampen their spirits. Heather Park was a magnificent property set within a substantial estate, but was only a short carriage ride from Heathfield. Nearby, were several other mansions and properties of note. Heathfield had the advantage of being close enough to the coast to benefit from the sea air that drifted inland to the English countryside. A brisk but fairly long walk would secure a view of the sea, while a gentle stroll in the countryside was on the Ashby family's doorstep. The best of both worlds.

Heather Park had no sea breeze, ensconced as it was in the heart of the lush countryside. Heather grew in patches of lilac, purple, white and pink that looked like they were quilted into the greenery.

Cottages were dotted throughout the estate, and the land itself invited those with a penchant for the beauties of cultured nature to visit and admire the estate. A ball being held at the prestigious Heather Park was indeed a jewel of an event on the social calendar.

But most of all, it offered the chance to meet with the new owner of Heather Park. The young, rich and eligible Sabastien Hunter. Mr. Hunter had recently inherited the estate from his late grandfather, and was the third unattached gentleman to recently become available in the neighbourhood.

'We now have three eligible gentlemen of fortune in our midst. I'm sure they'll all be at the ball. What a wonderful season this will be.' Mrs. Ashby had exalted hopes of at least one of her daughters securing an engagement before the summer was over.

Mr. Ashby frowned over the top of his newspaper. 'Three, you say?'

'Yes.' His wife sounded exasperated. 'I told you that Blackhall and Seaforth, both substantial houses as you well know, have recently been inherited or taken charge of.'

'I thought the admiral was still in residence at Seaforth,' Mr. Ashby said, wondering if he'd missed the gossip.

'The admiral has decided to take himself on a long voyage, sailing off to Europe or wherever the notion takes him,' Mrs. Ashby explained. 'His grandson, Domenic DeGrey, is the new resident. He's a naval captain himself. It's all very exciting.'

'Is my name on the invitation?' Annabel put her bread and jam aside and ran round to peer over her mother's shoulder. Both mother and daughter had lovely blue eyes and barley blonde hair. Annabel smiled in anticipation as she skim read the letter.

'All our names are listed,' Mrs. Ashby assured Annabel. 'It's a truly personal invitation.' She looked at her husband, wishing his enthusiasm equalled her own, but he continued to eat his egg, spread butter on a thick cut slice of bread, and read his newspaper. This was no indication that he wasn't happy that his wife and daughters had a ball to look forward to, rather it was the realisation that he wouldn't be able to attend.

'Mr. Ashby! Are you not delighted for us?' his wife demanded, eyes bright and smiling at him.

He folded his newspaper and put it aside. He had a tall, lean build and strong posture that gave him an air of fatherly authority. 'I must remind you that I am due to travel to Bath on business, and will not be able to attend the ball.'

It took all her restraint for Mrs. Ashby to refrain from telling him to postpone his trip, but she knew that it was important financially. As a family, they were well–to–do, not well–off, and certainly not rich. Not like the bestower of the invitation, Mr. Hunter.

Evelyn spoke up, trying to hide her disappointment. The date of the ball did indeed clash with her father's trip to Bath, and she had insisted he take her with him. He'd only recently agreed, so although she secretly wanted to attend the ball, she reluctantly decided to forgo it. 'I cannot go either. I'm set to travel with father.'

'But surely you'd prefer to go to the ball, Evelyn,' her mother said. 'You've long wanted to view inside Heather Park. Admire the paintings. Now you have a chance and you'd rather go to Bath.'

Evelyn sipped her tea, lowered her green eyes, and tried not to appear perturbed. Sunlight streaming through the windows highlighted her strawberry blonde hair and cast her in a warm glow that didn't match the bitter chill of her disappointment. 'There will be other balls.'

'Not like this one,' her mother was quick to reply. 'We'll all meet Mr. Hunter and the other gentlemen are sure to have been invited. There's never been a time when three wealthy and eligible young men, from three different houses, have all become available for—'

'Marrying?' Mr. Ashby cut–in, straightening his paper as he picked it up again.

'There's nothing wrong with hoping that at least one of our daughters will find a suitable husband this summer.' Mrs. Ashby adjusted herself, like a hen fluffing its feathers. 'According to Lady Thornbee and a few other close acquaintances I've spoken to recently, the gentlemen are all handsome.'

'And rich,' Mr. Ashby added.

'And amiable,' Mrs. Ashby told him. 'I am reliably informed that all three are invariably well dressed, gentile mannered, and excel at various activities including fencing, dancing and riding. All are suitably equipped to make ideal husbands.' She fanned herself with a napkin. 'It's almost too wonderful to contemplate.'

'Well then,' Mr. Ashby said, 'perhaps there is some sort of compromise. Maybe Evelyn and I could go with you to attend the ball, for a couple of hours, but leave early enough to then travel. We could travel overnight and wake up in Bath the next morning. Evelyn, you could sleep in the carriage, couldn't you?'

'Yes.' She could sleep anywhere if it allowed her to go to the ball and to Bath. She got up and hugged her father. 'Thank you.'

'You must write immediately of our acceptance to Mr. Hunter,' Mrs. Ashby implored her husband.

'I shall, my dear,' Mr. Ashby confirmed, once more enjoying his breakfast now that the matter had been decided. There would be little else left but for the chatter to recommence, and he anticipated the excited topic of it.

Mr. Ashby had initially wished for a son, but now resigned himself to being the only man in the family. His wealthy and much–loved brother promised to secure their house, Heathfield, on Mr. Ashby's passing, thereby providing continued security for his wife and girls. However, Mr. Ashby was of stout constitution and planned to reach a ripe old age while providing for his family. His business brought in a fair amount of money, and as an astute dealer in finance and investment, he knew how to economise on frivolities while being somewhat lavish with his wife and daughters. Pretty dresses, ribbons and lace, could send them into a tizzy of excitement that no economising could contest with. He was quite content with his library of books in his study, though the door was never fully closed and the skipping and bustling intrusions from Mrs. Ashby and his girls was wholly welcome.

'What shall we wear?' Primrose asked, wondering if the dress she'd been sewing recently was fitting for such a grand occasion. Primrose had summer blonde hair and pale grey eyes. All three sisters were considered pretty to beautiful depending on the person delivering the compliment.

'Your new dress would be perfect,' Mrs. Ashby said encouragingly. 'Such pretty white fabric, and the pale yellow primroses you embroidered on the neckline are lovely. Those trims you added are so fashionable. Wear your velvet cloak with it,' she advised.

Trips to London and excursions to other towns were their source of the latest fashions. Gleaning the styles of dresses worn by those in fashionable circles enabled them to sew equivalent dresses of their own. Fabric was the main cost, but Mr. Ashby was generous with their dressmaking allowances, and had never complained if extra embellishment of silk, velvet or lace was purchased to enhance the final garment and render it fashionable.

Mrs. Ashby was a skilled seamstress and loved nothing better than sitting in the parlour stitching in the company of her daughters. They shared their mother's love of sewing, embroidery, quilting and all forms of needlework, and all three daughters had learned to adjust patterns, and fit and finish garments to a high degree. Mr. Ashby benefited from their skills and the silk back waistcoats they made for him were often envied or remarked upon by other gentlemen. Not a hem of his jackets or shirt collar was ever unsuitable. Their love of fussing over his appearance was outmatched only by his love of their caring.

Evelyn shared her love of dressmaking with the paintings she created. Two of her paintings hung in her father's study. He never tired of admiring both artworks — fine watercolours.

Evelyn's artistic talents were employed for her own amusement, but frequently were gifted to friends and relatives.

Mr. Ashby's favourite view from the window of his study where he sat behind his desk, was the current project Evelyn was working on.

After breakfast, Evelyn left the bubbling activity in the house and seated herself outside with her watercolours, and set about finishing the painting for her father. The light at this time in the morning was at its most flattering to the scene. The house sat within a garden where flowers grew in profusion, and beyond them the grass and trees provided the perfect landscape. Sunlight filtered through the branches and for a moment she gazed up, then closed her eyes and let it dance upon her face.

The parlour windows were open and the voices of her mother and sisters wafted out to her in the clear morning air, allowing Evelyn to be part of their excited conversation while she painted.

'Evelyn!' Mrs. Ashby called to her. 'Do you have enough white ribbons for your dress and hair? We're making a list of things we need for the ball from the linen draper's shop.'

'I believe I have plenty of ribbon in my sewing box,' Evelyn called back to her mother.

Mrs. Ashby bustled over to Evelyn's sewing box. Each of the girls had their own box. Something Mrs. Ashby ensured. Sewing was not only a popular pastime in the Ashby household, it provided a practical benefit for making new linen, and mending well–worn items and restoring them to use.

Evelyn was skilled at picking apart a dress and redesigning it according to the latest fashion. A skill she'd learned from her mother, an expert in dressmaking and all sorts of needlework.

Designing bonnets and shawls was a favourite of Annabel, while Primrose loved anything of a floral nature pattern. When her parents named her Primrose little did they know she'd grow up to have a love for flowers to the extent that she embroidered little else.

All the women were avid embroiderers and their sewing boxes were filled with a selection of thread, needles, pins, scissors and necessary items for their embroidery and dressmaking. The boxes contained drawers and compartments where notes and individual keepsakes were kept. Primrose had a stash of floral embroidery patterns, while Mrs. Ashby, Evelyn and Annabel had between them a wide variety of patterns folded and tucked away in the sewing boxes.

Some patterns were cut and kept from magazines, but mainly they were the design of Mrs. Ashby whose collection had been build up over the years and encompassed everything they really needed. These were updated according to the latest fashions.

For their embroidery patterns the women were spoiled because Evelyn could draw whatever flowers, butterflies, bees, birds and other creatures for the designs they wanted. It was now rare for them to embroider any patterns other than those based on Evelyn's beautiful artwork. Everything from bluebells, pansies, roses and lily of the valley to lovely butterflies, dragonflies and robins adorned the household linen and clothes. The embroidery was perfect for adding a fashionable flair to their dresses, rendering them unique. The Ashby women's dresses were often admired for their flourishes at social events. Now, with the Heather Park ball upon them, their skills were in fine demand.

'Yes, Evelyn, you have plenty of white ribbon,' Mrs. Ashby called out to her. 'But I think you need more embroidery thread. I'll make sure to buy your favourite colours from the linen draper's shop.'

Evelyn relayed her thanks to her mother and continued with her watercolour painting. The light was wonderful that morning.

Three of the trees, those nearest the house, were beautiful. Older than the house itself, they created a canopy of leaves and branches, and their wide trunks were covered in moss so verdant that Evelyn felt she couldn't quite capture it. She sighed and resigned herself to painting the luminosity of the moss with her truest green watercolours.

An hour or two passed and she felt...yes, the painting was complete as it ever would be. She breathed in the heady air, a mix of greenery, flowers and a hint of the sea. Having been sitting for so long, she was tempted to go for a walk, an activity she invariably enjoyed, and headed happily towards the sea.

Meanwhile, Mrs. Ashby, Annabel and Primrose had walked into the nearby town to shop for trimmings and thread.

Evelyn hoped they'd buy extra white thread for the whitework embroidery on the new evening dress she planned to wear to the ball. She might even add some goldwork to the design for such a special occasion. The design was almost finished, and she aimed to work on it later in the day. Touches of embroidery were on most of her dresses, including the day dress she was wearing. It was fashioned from light cream cotton, embroidered with bluebells, and was worn with a short jacket and comfortable ankle boots. A harsh winter that stretched long into the spring had resulted in her figure being very much on the slender side. But her good posture strengthened her appearance.

The countryside had a glow of summer, and there were times when Evelyn felt as if she was walking through one of the watercolours she'd painted of this verdant landscape. Fields stretched far and wide, and there were pockets of trees and wooded areas, like the one she was now in, where the scent of the trees mingled with the warm, summery air. Some of the trees had roots so gnarled she had to pick her way over them, and often she would sit there, shaded by their leaves on hot days, to admire the view, breathe in the heady aroma, and ponder about her life and her family.

She ventured on, gazing up at the clear blue sky, feeling the benefit of her walk through the countryside. Her long hair, pinned up at the sides, shone in the sunshine. By the end of the summertime the sunlight would've stolen the strawberry red tones within the pale blonde strands and created a sun lightened beauty to one of her main assets. Evelyn's hair was a statement of her personality. Cool headed with fiery streaks.

Evelyn continued to walk on, her thoughts drifting to the excitement of the ball...so deep in thought, she didn't hear the man approach...

A man on horseback, a newcomer she did not recognise, startled her as he rode across her path. He was well–dressed, in his twenties, with dark hair and a foreboding countenance.

He immediately pulled up and apologised. 'I beg your pardon.' His voice was rich, deep and resonated through the calm air, but created a stir in her.

His green eyes, set in an extraordinarily handsome face, viewed her thoughtfully. 'May I be so bold as to enquire if you have lost your way or are in need of assistance?'

She gazed at him with wide green eyes that were a fair match for his in intensity. 'No, thank you, sir. I am quite fine.'

The dark, sweeping brows arched in curiosity, encouraging an explanation, a reason for wandering so far from anywhere. She was a fair distance from the sea, and in the depths of the countryside. A young lady alone.

'I am walking to the sea. I do this fairly often, so thank you for concern, but I am fine,' she assured him.

He nodded, and she noticed the breadth of his shoulders beneath his dark jacket, and the strength of his long thighs clad in fawn breeches. His boots were polished to a high degree, and he had an air of authority about him.

'I'll bid you good day then.' He almost said something else, thought better of it, and then rode off.

His skills in horsemanship were evident from the manner in which he navigated the route through the trees, guiding his magnificent chestnut horse into the thick of it with ease.

Soon, he was gone, and she felt an unfamiliar disappointment, that she may never know who this handsome and gallant stranger was or encounter him again.

Shrugging off such an indulgent notion, she ventured on until she reached the coast.

The sea sparkled far into the distance, and she wondered if she would one day sail out to where it faded into a dazzling row of sunbeams. Men's adventures teased her often, and she tried not to reveal her bitterness that women were not allowed to indulge their adventurous spirits the way men were. It was unfair. She sighed, and pushed these thoughts away to admire the scintillating sea and breathe in the fresh air.

In the distance stood Seaforth, a mansion overlooking the coast. It always gave her the impression it faced the force of the sea with such defiance that it added to its character. It suited an admiral or navy gentleman. But she still preferred the homeliness of Heathfield.

Captain Domenic DeGrey rode on until he couldn't stand the hurt he felt any longer. As if his heart had been thoroughly torn. He pulled the reins, stopped and dismounted from his horse. His breathing was ragged and he tried to steady himself.

Of all the women to encounter, it had to be Evelyn Ashby!

She was even more beautiful than he remembered.

For the past four years he'd wondered if his thoughts of her were unrealistic. The seventeen–year–old beauty he'd secretly admired from afar was now the young woman he'd long hoped for. Four years away at sea in the British Navy, and he'd thought of no other woman except her.

He breathed heavily, disappointed by his new predicament. He'd aimed to hold a ball at Seaforth and plans were already underway. But the impromptu ball at Heather Park had beaten him to it. He'd received his invitation that morning from Mr. Hunter, a man he'd never met, and planned to attend the ball in the hope of finally being formally introduced to Evelyn Ashby. Now their first meeting would be edged with a familiarity from their chance encounter. She'd recognise him as the man who'd almost trampled her while out riding.

If he decided to forgo the ball at Heather Park, and instead invite the Ashby family to a ball at Seaforth, as he'd originally intended, what if Miss Ashby decided not to accept? So, now he was forced to go to the Heather Park event, if he was to guarantee meeting her, be formally introduced, and realise his long held hopes of knowing her. And telling her that she was the reason he'd come home to Seaforth.

CHAPTER TWO

The town's main thoroughfare was bathed in mid–morning sunlight.

Mrs. Ashby, Annabel and Primrose walked towards the linen draper's shop. The bustling small town had a selection of shops that supplied the neighbourhood and surrounding areas. The gentle rumbling of carriages driving along were outmatched by the chatter of the townsfolk out shopping and going about their daily business.

As they approached, Mrs. Ashby saw Lady Thornbee and her nineteen–year–old daughter, Octavia.

'There's Lady Thornbee.' Mrs. Ashby waved and smiled.

Lady Thornbee nodded and smiled, while Octavia retained her haughty attitude undisturbed and walked alongside her mother. Octavia had inherited her rich chestnut hair and hazel eyes from her mother, but her aloof attitude was entirely her own.

All of them were heading to the linen draper's shop, as were a couple of other ladies, eager to purchase trimmings for their dresses.

'You received your invitation to the Heather Park ball I presume,' Lady Thornbee said to Mrs. Ashby as they met outside the shop.

'We did,' Mrs. Ashby confirmed brightly. 'My girls and I are so excited.'

'As are we.' Lady Thornbee sounded vaguely thrilled. 'Octavia is quite delighted.'

Octavia showed no hint of being thrilled or even mildly amused. But nowadays she rarely offered a smile never mind an entire display of elation.

It had been quietly suggested in the lower layers of gossip that since turning nineteen, Octavia had become too taken by her own beauty to deem it necessary to add to it by smiling.

Privately, and only to her own daughters, Mrs. Ashby surmised this was the result of Lady Thornbee's constant praise of her admittedly beautiful daughter. At seventeen she'd reached a high level of loveliness, but she did smile, and talked to others, including the Ashby women. Now though, Octavia had come to believe she was due the exalted future extolled by Lady Thornbee of marrying a man of fortune and securing a place in the upper echelons of society.

By default, Mrs. Ashby concluded, the girl's lack of smiles and fair manners detracted from her beauty far more than they added to it. However, as Octavia was to become a rival of Evelyn, Annabel and Primrose for the wealthiest partners, Mrs. Ashby viewed this as a benefit. Besides, in her eyes, there were none so beautiful than her own daughters, nor such pleasant company. Any man of fortune would surely prefer a woman with amiable manners and a cheerful attitude, as well as beauty, to a cold comeliness.

'I'm told the ball had little planning, decided on a whim by Mr. Hunter,' said Lady Thornbee.

'More notice would've been preferable,' Mrs. Ashby admitted. 'However, we have new dresses suitable for such a wonderful occasion.' She flicked a look at the shop's window display that was enticingly draped with fabric, ribbons, trimming, and baskets brimming with pretty adornments. 'We just need a handful of embellishments to complete their fine fashion.'

'Fashion, hmmm, yes...' Lady Thornbee mused. 'Such a fickle necessity.'

Annabel squeezed Primrose's arm and pointed to the new fabric and trimmings in the shop window. 'The shop has lots of new items,' she said, eager to go inside.

Primrose nodded enthusiastically. 'May I buy ribbon for a sash?' she asked her mother, eyeing the wide pale yellow satin ribbon, imagining it would be perfect to tie around the high waistline of her white ball gown. 'Enough for a bow and longer tails?'

Mrs. Ashby looked at the items in the window display, tempted by quite a few of them herself. 'Of course, let's all go in, shall we?'

Without lingering any longer, the Ashby ladies entered the shop, closely followed by Lady Thornbee and Octavia.

Annabel was the first to walk in, gasping as she encountered a young man of elegant styling on his way out. Head and shoulders taller than all of them, exceedingly well–dressed, with light brown hair and eyes to match, he gave way to the ladies and stood aside holding the door ajar while they passed him by.

His gentlemanly gesture was acknowledged by each of the women as they entered, but his expression brightened as Primrose brushed past him. His attention to her caused her to gaze up at him with her curious grey eyes.

Mrs. Ashby followed Primrose, and although he nodded to her politely, his eyes returned to look at Primrose and Annabel, but especially the former. A gesture that did not go unnoticed by Mrs. Ashby or Lady Thornbee.

Octavia was the last to enter, but even her beauty wasn't enough to detract from the instant impact Primrose had on him.

She was indeed a sweet young beauty to behold, he thought, and then caught himself before his diverted attention became uncomfortable and blatantly obvious.

As all the women were now in the shop, the man nodded politely and left. Mrs. Ashby and Lady Thornbee watched him walk past the shop window. He gave another glance in the window, and then disappeared along the way.

Mrs. Ashby raised her brows and exchanged a look with Lady Thornbee while the younger women made beelines for the new ribbons and trims, including the supposedly underwhelmed Octavia.

Lady Thornbee was known to the two women attending the shop. She spoke to the woman behind the counter while the other measured the hem of a lady's dress at the back of the shop during a personal dressmaking fitting. 'Do you know the name of that gentleman?'

'Yes, Lady Thornbee,' the shop assistant replied. 'That is Mr. Gilles London.'

'I've never heard of him. Is he of local acquaintance?'

'He said he's from Bath, here to attend the ball at Heather Park. An acquaintance of Mr. Sabastien Hunter. He mentioned that he's staying at the Horse Shoe.' The shop assistant indicated towards the inn further along from the way.

'Not a close acquaintance obviously, or he'd be staying as a guest at Heather Park rather than the Horse Shoe,' Lady Thornbee scoffed.

'So Mr. London will be attending the ball?' said Mrs. Ashby.

The shop assistant nodded. 'Yes, he saw the new cravats for gentlemen that we have in the window. He said he wanted one for the ball.'

Annabel and Primrose hurried over to see the cravats on display. Only a few were left in the window. The shop didn't usually stock cravats, but these were temporarily available, made from white linen.

'These are very nice,' said Annabel. 'Do you think we could buy one for father?'

Mrs. Ashby ventured to have a peek, and nodded. 'Certainly. I think he would like this one.' She picked it up and placed it on the shop counter as the first item she was set to purchase.

Annabel and Primrose agreed, happy that they'd surprise their father with a gift from the shop. So often they only purchased items for themselves, so it was pleasing to include him in their shopping.

Lady Thornbee remained thoughtful. 'Mr. London was quite taken with Primrose.'

Primrose subdued a blush, and brushed this notion aside. 'I'm sure I didn't notice him pay any special attention to me.' She glanced at Octavia whose hazel eyes were deep with envy.

Octavia acknowledged Mr. London's good looks, but was puzzled as to why he'd barely noticed her. The thought that he was too taken with Primrose to notice little else didn't sit easy with her. She began to sift through a selection of ribbons with slight annoyance. But if Gilles London did attend the forthcoming ball, she would make sure he noticed her then.

Lady Thornbee confided to Mrs. Ashby while their daughters browsed around the shop. 'I hear there is another ball in the planning.'

'Another ball, in the neighbourhood?'

'Yes, but Sabastien Hunter's decision to hold one at Heather Park has hindered their plans.'

'Where is the other ball being held?'

'At Seaforth.'

Mrs. Ashby blinked. 'Seaforth? I don't remember there ever being a ball at Seaforth.'

'No, the admiral wasn't one for holding events, but now that his grandson, Captain Domenic DeGrey, is in charge of Seaforth, a ball is to be held there fairly soon.' Lady Thornbee kept her voice to a whisper. 'Captain DeGrey is said to be of a sociable nature and will be at the Heather Park ball, so we'll have a chance to meet him. He's done well for himself in the navy, and has his own wealth, in addition to whatever fortune his grandfather has left him.'

Mrs. Ashby took in the details of this latest gossip. 'Another ball would be very pleasing.'

'Another ball?' Annabel piped up, overhearing her mother. 'Where? When?'

'Hush,' Mrs. Ashby scolded her.

Octavia spoke up. 'A ball at Seaforth. Captain DeGrey is planning this soon.'

'How exciting,' Annabel said, exchanging an enthusiastic smile with Primrose.

'We'll need other dresses for the second ball,' said Primrose.

'Octavia has a few new dresses for such occasions,' Lady Thornbee said with a satisfied smile.

'We'll make what we need,' Mrs. Ashby assured her daughters, and then eyed the fabric available. From fine linen, muslin, dress cotton, silk, satin and georgette, they were spoiled for choice.

The fabric was selected, mainly white, though two light colours were included — the palest lemon and pastel pink.

Lady Thornbee didn't entirely approve of the pastel colours. 'White is always preferable for a ball. It gives the skin such luminosity, a glow in the candlelight and lamp light. Though if I had to select a pastel shade it would be lemon or pink, never blue or green. They can make a lady's complexion appear quite sallow.'

Mrs. Ashby reconsidered her fabric choice. 'Yes, you're right, white is always so flattering to the complexion.'

'I like the lemon colour,' Primrose said firmly, 'Anyone attending both balls will then know I had different dresses.'

Mrs. Ashby nodded. 'Yes, and the lemon is so light as to have just a hint of colour.' She held the fabric up to the light. 'I think it will give your skin a wonderful pale golden glow.'

'My heart's set on the pink, mama,' Annabel added.

Deciding to stick with the original choices, Mrs. Ashby bought the white fabric and both pastels.

Ribbons and trims were purchased along with the dressmaking fabric, and the women continued to chat while they shopped.

'What will you wear if there's a third ball?' Octavia asked Annabel, certain that she wouldn't have a suitable response.

Annabel was quick to reply. 'I'll wear the white dress again and accessorise it with different ribbons and embroidery.' She eyed Octavia defiantly. 'I'm sure that any gentlemen attending the other events wouldn't despise a lady for wearing the same dress. And if he did, he'd show himself to be of poor character, and I'd pay him no attention at all.'

Lady Thornbee didn't want any animosity. 'Let's agree not to quarrel over the attention of any single gentlemen we may or may not become acquainted with. From everything I've heard, there will be quite a few eligible young men of fortune in the neighbourhood over the coming weeks. The summer season is set to be very exciting.'

All the women agreed, except Octavia. She busied herself at the ribbons.

Mrs. Ashby and her daughters added embroidery thread to their purchases, and included white thread for Evelyn.

'Evelyn will need extra embroidery thread for her whitework,' said Mrs. Ashby.

At the mention of Evelyn's name, Octavia bristled. Evelyn's beauty had increased in the past few years, rather than faded. If anyone was her rival in looks, it was Evelyn. Annabel's bloom was still on the rise, she supposed, and Primrose had become quite lovely. But it was always Evelyn that she'd secretly envied for her natural beauty and artistic flair. Octavia liked to embroider, but she relied on patterns from magazines or those purchased from the fabric draper's shop. She would never stoop to embroidering Evelyn's floral designs no matter if she really wanted to.

On the shop counter was a basket filled with off–cuts, small pieces of fabric left over from larger cuts. These were recommended to be sewn into reticules, small bags, ideal for evening events. The fabrics included pieces of velvet, satin and linen.

Mrs. Ashby added several of these bargain pieces to her purchases.

'What are you going to make with those?' Lady Thornbee asked her.

'Bags. I have a design that works for little pieces like these. Evelyn's floral designs are easily embroidered on to enhance the bag's prettiness.'

Lady Thornbee eyed the fabric remnants. 'Perhaps I could have a copy of your bag design?'

'Of course,' said Mrs. Ashby. 'I'd be happy to give you the pattern.'

Lady Thornbee was wealthy enough to afford to buy her own bags, but she enjoyed sewing, and it helped pass the long days and evenings alone without her husband. Lord Thornbee was often abroad for months on end, being a great man and doing great things. She wasn't always sure what these things were exactly, but he was a diplomat of sorts and travelled to distant lands to attend to whatever matters required his intelligence and diplomacy.

With their purchases complete, they all left the shop together and chatted for a moment outside.

'I'll have someone pop over with a copy of the bag pattern for you,' Mrs. Ashby promised.

As they smiled and went to go their separate ways, the tall figure of Mr. Gilles London walked towards them. He nodded politely, smiled, glanced at Primrose, and then headed on.

'Coincidence or deliberate?' Lady Thornbee said of the encounter.

'The latter I think,' Mrs. Ashby said with a knowing smile.

'I believe the ball is going to prove to be very interesting,' Lady Thornbee added, before they all headed off in different directions.

'Did you see the way he looked at you?' Annabel whispered to Primrose.

'I know,' Primrose agreed, and then giggled as she walked alongside Annabel and her mother.

The Ashby women sat in the parlour engrossed in two things — sewing and conversation. Two pastimes that could be enjoyed together without one disturbing the other. Mrs. Ashby was so accustomed to chatting while stitching, she found herself almost inclined to talk to herself when her daughters were busy elsewhere. On those occasions, she'd pick up her embroidery or whatever she was working on, and join Mr. Ashby in his study and chat to him. If it ever tired him, he never said, but she was inclined to think that even after all the years they'd been together, they were still fond of the other's company. She'd loved none but him, and so it always was. An assurance matched by Mr. Ashby's devotion to his wife.

Mrs. Ashby and her daughters had been busy sewing all afternoon, and after dinner were stitching well into the night by the glow of candlelight.

Small embroideries were framed and hung in sets on the parlour walls. A fritillary, foxglove and fairy lantern flower adorned the wall on one side of the fireplace, while gypsophila, heliotrope, lilac and lavender were hung on the other side, along with a floral watercolour painted by Evelyn.

A little embroidered gardenia tree, cherry and strawberry blossom were framed near the window. Depending on the season, these were hung in other rooms in the house where they could be admired on rotation. New embroideries replaced older versions, sometimes in keeping with fashion or simply frivolity in decor. It gave a purpose to their embroideries as well as pleasure from viewing them.

The girls' samplers, embroidered years ago when they were first leaning each embroidery stitch — from satin stitch to backstitch, to chain stitch and stem stitch, were framed on the far wall. The samplers were a handy reference for all of them to refer to when deciding on stitches for their patterns. Their names were embroidered along the edge of each sampler, and it was interesting to note that all three had such individual styles and tastes in colours and stitching, even though they'd all learned from the skilled hands of Mrs. Ashby.

But that was the beauty of embroidery, Mrs. Ashby had long told them. One pattern worked by different embroiderers looked unlike the others. Thus, she emphasised, patterns could be shared while still providing individual creativity.

Reticules, the elegant small bags suitable to take to the ball, were being finished — embroidered with flowers and embellished with beads that added a shimmer for their evening use. A sunflower was emblazoned on Annabel's bag. Evelyn had drawn a butterfly on the flower, creating an interesting design that was a pleasure to embroider.

Primrose's bag had a daisy and primrose design embroidered on it with white, pale yellow and muted green thread. A scattering of tiny beads made it look like little bees were buzzing around the flowers. It was the most attractive bag she'd ever sewn.

The whitework embroidery on Evelyn's bag included a daisy fleabane with a dragonfly on the flower. Evelyn was busy stitching gold thread on to the work to enrich the design. The thread glittered under the beeswax candle that she sat beside to do her sewing. The beeswax candles barely dripped, so there was little chance of it ruining the embroidery that rested underneath it. Evelyn loved the glowing light the candles produced, reminding her of sunlight.

Evelyn had finished the whitework embroidery she'd added to her father's new cravat. They'd decided to give it a stylish leaf design and she'd included a tiny bee. Mr. Ashby was busy in his study, and they intended giving him the gift later that evening.

Meanwhile, they were chatting about Mr. Gilles London and wondering about the handsome and gallant stranger Evelyn had spoken to earlier that day.

'He might turn up at the ball,' said Annabel. 'He could be visiting here, like Mr. London, to attend the ball.'

'He could,' Evelyn agreed. 'I just wish we knew more about Mr. Hunter. We're attending a ball at Heather Park and yet we barely know anything about him. Didn't Lady Thornbee tell you anything?'

'She knows only that he's the grandson of Sir Hunter,' said Mrs. Ashby. 'Apart from being the new owner of Heather Park, we'll have to find out all about him at the ball.'

Primrose smiled. 'I quite like the intrigue of it all.'

'Sabastien Hunter sounds rather mysterious,' said Annabel.

Mrs. Ashby finished stitching her bag and began tidying things away in her sewing box. 'I've never known a time when there were so many eligible young men in the neighbourhood.'

'But there will be plenty of young women vying for their attention,' Evelyn reminded her mother.

Mrs. Ashby tilted her chin up defiantly. 'Yes, but I think you will all find yourselves in great demand with gentlemen wanting to dance with you.'

'Lady Thornbee seems set on securing a partner for Octavia,' Annabel commented.

'She does,' Mrs. Ashby agreed. 'But as I've said, her lack of smiles and pleasant manner diminish her beauty.' She became thoughtful. 'I think she misses her father. Lord Thornbee is hardly ever at home these days. I've given up asking Lady Thornbee if he's home from his adventures abroad.'

'I'd hate it if papa was away,' said Primrose.

The others nodded.

‘I remember Octavia years ago,’ said Annabel. ‘She used to love her father dearly and was always happy when he was around. Perhaps that’s why she’s so miserable nowadays. She misses him.’

Mrs. Ashby sighed. ‘I don’t envy Lady Thornbee. She’s rich, but we manage very well, and I’d rather have less money, but the assurance of the company of my husband.’ She shuddered and pulled her shawl around her shoulders. ‘I couldn’t settle if Mr. Ashby was often away. I wouldn’t like that at all.’

‘I’m glad to hear it,’ Mr. Ashby said, walking into the room, overhearing their conversation.

Mrs. Ashby pursed her lips at him. ‘Mr. Ashby! One day you will hear something about yourself that you will not like. And it’ll be your own fault for sneaking around.’

He smiled at her. ‘I trust my character is in safe hands with you my dear.’

Mrs. Ashby smiled back at him.

Evelyn signalled to her mother. They’d planned to give him the cravat.

Mrs. Ashby nodded at Evelyn.

Taking the carefully folded cravat from her sewing box where she’d hidden it from view, Evelyn stood up. ‘We have something for you.’

Mr. Ashby looked surprised. ‘Something for me?’ He glanced at all the sewing strewn around the room — dresses, bags and other items.

The women were smiling as Evelyn handed him the cravat.

At first, he didn’t know what it was.

‘We hope you like it, papa,’ said Evelyn.

He unfolded the gift and his face lit up with joy. ‘A new cravat! Did you make it?’

‘We bought it at the shop when we were buying fabric,’ Mrs. Ashby explained. ‘Another gentleman, Mr. Gilles London, bought one and we decided to buy one for you. Evelyn has embroidered it for you.’

He studied the whitework she’d embroidered on the cravat. ‘It’s exceptional, thank you all so much. And thank you, Evelyn, for the embroidery work.’

Evelyn pointed to the bee. ‘I included a bee. I know you like bees.’

'I do, yes. This is lovely. I'll wear it to the ball.'

The women were delighted that Mr. Ashby was happy with his gift, and then they all started to get ready for bed. The sewing was put away tidily, and the candles extinguished.

The dresses they'd all been embroidering, or adding trimmings to, were hung in the wardrobes to keep them pristine for the ball.

There was a bedroom for each of the girls upstairs in the house, but Evelyn and Annabel shared a room, as they liked to chat before going to sleep, and enjoyed each other's company. Their single beds faced each other, and it was usually Evelyn's task to blow out the candle by her bedside when they went to sleep.

Evelyn fluffed her pillow, swept her long plaited hair out of the way, and blew out the flame.

The scent of the candle was still in the air after being extinguished, when Annabel spoke up in the shadowed darkness. 'Do you think there's something suspicious about Mr. London?'

'His interest in Primrose, you mean?'

'Yes. He seems quite fine, and we obviously don't know him, but...' Annabel sighed. 'There's something about him that makes me wonder about his intentions. I think he deliberately walked past us when we came out of the shop today. So he must've been watching for us. A true gentleman wouldn't do that, or shouldn't do that.'

Evelyn agreed. 'We'll make sure he doesn't do anything improper to upset Primrose.'

Their decision made, they settled down and went to sleep.

CHAPTER THREE

The Ashby family were dressed in their finery as their carriage drove up to the ball. Flaming torches lit up the night, burning along the driveway leading to the spectacular house. Heather Park stood aglow in the evening light, a welcoming sight, as the carriage pulled up and they stepped out into the calm night air.

Evelyn felt the fluttering of excitement as she gazed up at the house, the largest in the neighbourhood, a classic building with a front entrance buzzing with guests arriving for the ball in their carriages. She smoothed the fabric of her white dress that was embroidered with floral whitework and tiny dragonflies with a hint of goldwork. Her hair was pinned up and secured with a sparkling clasp. Wearing long white gloves, embroidered with a floral design, she clutched the small bag she'd made and walked towards the house with her family. Her sisters and mother chattered excitedly, and although she felt equally thrilled, she let their voices filter into the night air while she quietly followed along with her father. As promised, he wore the cravat, and she was pleased with how well it suited him.

Everyone was dressed to impress, with the ladies in their beautiful dresses, with glittering clasps, pearls and adornments pinned in their upswept hair. Some had ringlets framing their faces, or long curls worn over one shoulder, carefully entwined with tiny jewels. All the goldwork, jewels and beading on their dresses, gloves, low heeled shoes and bags sparkled like scattered starlight in the night. Jewellery itself was understated. The Ashby ladies wore no necklaces, earrings or bracelets of any kind. Their dresses and accessories provided all the shimmer needed.

The chatter swirled around Evelyn, a mix of anticipation and awe.

Gentlemen were aplenty. Tailcoats, waistcoats and cravats tied in numerous styles were the mainstay of their evening wear. Dark tones of black, grey, navy and burgundy were prominent, though lighter creams and ecru were also favoured. Shirts and cravats were white or cream, the knots showing each gentleman's preference for classic or fashionable styles.

Mr. Sabastien Hunter stood within the vast entrance that was thronging with people, greeting his guests as they arrived. The waterfall styling of his white cravat was the most ornate item he wore. His tailcoat was black and his shirt white. His satin waistcoat was all but hidden under his buttoned up tailcoat, but the edge showed beneath the coat's waist length front, a hint of stylish taste. Although his face was stern, even as he welcomed guests, he was incredibly handsome, in his twenties, with sapphire blue eyes and rich dark hair. Sculptured features gave him a classic handsomeness.

Evelyn's first glimpse of him caught her off guard. Shielded by the outstretched arms of Mr. Ashby, he ushered his ladies towards the host, waiting until it was their turn to be properly introduced. He handed the invitation to the member of staff to make the announcement.

As a couple in front of her stepped aside, Evelyn saw Mr. Hunter, nodding politely to guests, his attention on them. But suddenly he flicked a glance in her direction, as if something had stirred the air. An anticipation of their meeting, a feeling that made her heart squeeze just looking at him.

Those sapphire eyes cut past everyone in the crowded space, looking only at her, the woman he'd never met and did not know whatsoever. And then he looked away, giving his full attention to the guests nearest him.

'I think Mr. Hunter noticed you, Evelyn,' her father whispered, leaning down protectively over her shoulder, still shielding them from being accidentally jostled. Everyone seemed to have arrived at the same time, causing an overspill of guests in the busy entrance.

Evelyn glanced up and round at her father. The look on her face acknowledged this was true. But why?

Before she had a chance to ponder this, they were standing in front of the exceedingly tall figure of Mr. Hunter. Broad shoulders tapered down to a lean waist emphasised by the fitted cut of his tailcoat. His long legs were clad in black trousers, and he wore shoes fit for dancing in. Evelyn thought that he was a fine figure of a man, probably the most strikingly handsome she'd ever met.

In the back of her mind she heard their names being spoken as they were introduced, but her heart was thundering in her chest as she bowed her head and then met his intense blue gaze up close. His skin was naturally light, but he looked as if he'd been outdoors, perhaps riding, in the sunshine, and this had brought a warm golden tone to his face. It was the only warmth she felt, except for a deeper feeling, accompanied by the incessant racing of her heart.

'Thank you for inviting us, Mr. Hunter,' extolled Mrs. Ashby, genuinely delighted. 'My daughters are so looking forward to dancing this evening. And my eldest daughter, Evelyn, has expressed a longing to view the paintings at Heather Park. She's a keen artist herself, very talented.'

Evelyn felt a blush rise in her cheeks as her mother continued to praise her, especially as other guests were queuing up to be introduced.

'We should move along, my dear,' Mr. Ashby said to his wife, politely attempting to usher them towards the ballroom.

But Mr. Hunter's comment halted their leaving as he addressed Mrs. Ashby, while flicking glances at Evelyn. 'I would be happy for Miss Ashby to view the paintings at her leisure.'

'Thank you, Mr. Hunter,' said Mrs. Ashby, and then allowed herself to be escorted away by her husband.

Evelyn felt Mr. Hunter's gaze burn into her back as she walked with her family into the magnificent ballroom. As she entered, she couldn't resist glancing back over her shoulder, and there, through all the people, were those eyes watching her. He looked away immediately knowing he'd been caught staring at her, and she continued into the ballroom, feeling the need to link arms with her father. He smiled down at her, patted her hand, happy that they were there at the ball.

The room was vast, with alabaster coloured walls and an ornate ceiling, and crystal chandeliers and glass candelabras alight with beeswax candles illuminating the stylish decor. Generations of accumulated wealth and tastes in classic art and decor had resulted in an opulence that could only be achieved over decades.

An array of food was provided, along with attentive staff serving refreshments. In all the excitement of getting ready for the ball, the Ashby family hadn't eaten dinner, intending to have something to eat when they arrived.

'What did you think of Mr. Hunter?' Annabel asked her mother. Annabel's white dress enhanced her lovely figure, and she wore a scattering of pearls in her upswept hair.

'He seemed very elegant,' said Mrs. Ashby. 'And very handsome.'

'I thought he was aloof,' Primrose added.

'These rich men are often rather aloof,' Mrs. Ashby explained to Primrose. 'When I first met Mr. Ashby at a ball, I thought he would never ask me to dance because he expressed such a sense of self importance.'

'I was wondering how to ask you, my dear,' said Mr. Ashby. 'The moment I saw her,' he continued to explain to his daughters, 'I knew my heart was quite taken.'

Evelyn smiled at her father. 'I hope to have even half the happiness of you and mama.'

'Then I suggest we refrain from complaining about Mr. Hunter's aloofness,' Mrs. Ashby told them and then gestured around. 'Look at all the fine, young gentlemen here that you may meet.'

None of them noticed one of those gentlemen, Captain DeGrey, standing on the far side of the room, admiring Evelyn, and wondering if he could find a way to be formally introduced to her and her family. Unfortunately, he knew no one at the ball. Or at least, no one he recognised. He held a drink in his hand, untouched, a mere prop to make him look like he belonged at the ball, while all the while he felt apart from everyone. He wore a dark navy blue tailcoat and dark trousers with a white shirt and cravat knotted neatly. Even without his naval uniform, he cut a tall and commanding figure.

He watched as a gentleman approached the Ashby ladies, looking like he intended asking one of them to dance. One in particular — Primrose.

Primrose's dress was enhanced with the light yellow ribbon tied around the high waist of her white dress. Like her sisters, she wore her hair up, and had added a glittering clasp as a pretty accessory. Her long white gloves had buttons along the side and her bag hung from her wrist with ribbon.

'Good evening,' Mr. Gilles London said, hoping to introduce himself. He wore the white cravat he'd bought and a dark tailcoat and trousers.

Mr. Ashby spoke up. 'Good evening, Mr....?'

'Gilles London,' he said, bowing his head and smiling.

'We're delighted to make your acquaintance, Mr. London,' said Mrs. Ashby. 'This is Mr. Ashby, my husband, and my daughters, Evelyn, Annabel and Primrose.'

They all nodded acknowledgement.

'I believe we saw each other in town, at the linen draper's shop,' he said, prompting Mrs. Ashby.

'We did indeed,' Mrs. Ashby confirmed with a smile. Her dress was creamy white with a preponderance of lace and enhanced by the trimmings they'd purchased.

'I trust you found your purchases suitable,' Mr. London commented.

Primrose showed him her bag. 'We made reticules from the fabric pieces.'

Mr. London admired the embroidery on the bag. 'Very fine embroidery work I must say.'

'My sister, Evelyn, designed the pattern,' Primrose told him.

Mr. London turned his attention to Evelyn. 'A wonderful design.'

Evelyn smiled politely.

Mrs. Ashby spoke up. 'Evelyn is an accomplished artist.'

While they continued with their polite conversation, Captain DeGrey was making his way towards them, putting on a spurt of speed when he saw the man talking to Evelyn.

Before Captain DeGrey could reach them, Mr. London had asked Primrose to dance and been accepted. He led her on to the dance floor, causing Evelyn and Annabel to exchange a wary look.

By now, Mr. Ashby had decided to head over to the food and refreshments, encouraging his wife, Evelyn and Annabel to go with him. They passed Captain DeGrey on their way.

Evelyn shot him a look, recognising him instantly. She squeezed Annabel's hand, signalling to her.

Annabel caught the look and sensed that this was the gallant horseman Evelyn had encountered, but the moment was so fast that they had walked past him by the time the recognition had occurred.

Unsure what to do, Captain DeGrey made a bold move. 'I hope you enjoyed your walk to the coast.'

Evelyn turned and smiled at him. 'I did, sir.'

He bowed and introduced himself. There was nothing else for it. 'May I introduce myself? I'm Captain Domenic DeGrey.'

'DeGrey?' Mrs. Ashby's voice sounded shrill as she realised the connection. 'Admiral DeGrey's grandson?'

'That is correct, Mrs. Ashby,' he confirmed, and surprised her by knowing her name.

'Are you taking up permanent residence at Seaforth?' Mr. Ashby asked, making pleasant conversation, and letting the captain know he knew about the house.

'I am, for the foreseeable future,' Captain DeGrey told him. 'Until things are settled at least.'

'Until your grandfather comes home?' Evelyn asked him.

His heart ached every time he gazed at her. 'Yes, and until I decide if I am to leave the navy.'

'To settle down at Seaforth?' Mrs. Ashby was quick to ask.

'It is my wish to settle down,' he confirmed.

None of them picked up on the feelings he had for Evelyn. Instead, they smiled and were pleased to have made his acquaintance, as was expected at a ball.

Sensing they were comfortable with him, he took a deep breath to ask Evelyn to dance with him, but his intention was interrupted by the arrival of Mr. Hunter.

'Miss Ashby,' he announced. 'Would you care to view the paintings in the drawing room? There are watercolours perhaps to your liking.'

Evelyn's interest sparked at the unexpected offer. Mr. Hunter's demeanour was still aloof, but she dearly wanted to view the artwork.

'I would like this very much, Mr. Hunter,' Evelyn confirmed.

It was then that he introduced the two people walking towards them. 'May I introduce my good friend, Rupert Feingold and his cousin, Miss Raine Feingold. They are here from London, staying at Heather Park for the summer.'

Rupert Feingold had a ready smile, and a happy manner that made him instantly welcome in their company. He was tall, though not as tall as Mr. Hunter, and was in his twenties. His eyes were a lively mix of green with flecks of gold and hazel, and he had golden blond hair, as had his beautiful and elegant nineteen–year–old cousin, Raine. There was a sense of wealth about them, from their fine clothes and attitude. Mr. Feingold wore pristine cream and white attire. His tailcoat was styled to be worn unbuttoned to show his expensive oyster satin, single breasted waistcoat. Being friends of Mr. Hunter was also an indication of the circles they mingled in, though there was no hint of aloofness from either of the Feingolds.

Captain DeGrey found himself being relegated to the outskirts of the conversation, and the moment was lost to ask Evelyn to dance. It was now inappropriate to interrupt the host when he was introducing his friends to the Ashby family. He would have to wait, bide his time until later. But the night was young.

While they all became acquainted, Annabel kept a careful eye on Primrose dancing with Mr. London. Primrose was smiling happily, and there was nothing to cause her concern, quite the opposite. But there was also nothing about them that appeared to be a suitable couple. They didn't match.

'I thought perhaps Miss Feingold could join us,' Mr. Hunter suggested, making sure they were accompanied as he showed Evelyn the art.

There was nothing Captain DeGrey could do as Evelyn was swept away by Mr. Hunter. He couldn't have forced himself into their company, and had no great interest in viewing the Heather Park art. His interest was as it had been for years — to win the heart of Evelyn Ashby.

'The artwork is exquisite, Mr. Hunter.' Evelyn walked around the drawing room admiring the paintings that included a small collection of watercolours.

'I'm hoping to persuade Miss Feingold to paint Heather Park for me,' Mr. Hunter revealed. 'Perhaps you can help me to encourage her,' he said to Evelyn.

'You paint?' Evelyn said to her, smiling.

'I do, though rather less well than Mr. Hunter's expectations.'

'My expectations are definitely within your capability,' he said to Miss Feingold, causing her to smile and blush.

'He seeks to flatter me beyond my merit,' Miss Feingold said lightly to Evelyn.

'I would think that Mr. Hunter is a fine judge of your accomplishments,' Evelyn responded, playing along with the light manner of the conversation.

'Miss Feingold had a suggestion,' he began. 'When I told her of your artistic accomplishments, she wondered if you'd care to join her one day to paint here at Heather Park.'

'I would love your company, Miss Ashby,' she said before Evelyn could respond. 'You're clearly an accomplished artist if your embroidery designs are an indication of your talent.'

Evelyn's face lit up at the thought of painting at Heather Park. 'I'd be delighted. I dearly love to paint.'

'That's settled then,' Miss Feingold said, nodding firmly. 'The weather is quite fine at the moment. Perhaps you'd care to come along tomorrow or the day after? We could paint outdoors in the sunshine.' She flicked a teasing glance at Mr. Hunter. 'I may even attempt to paint Heather Park. Or maybe we both could?' she said to Evelyn.

The thought of painting Heather Park made Evelyn smile with joy. 'Yes, but unfortunately I am leaving this evening to travel to Bath with my father. But we will be back soon, within a few days.'

Miss Feingold smiled. 'Let me know when you come home, and we'll set a day for painting.'

Evelyn smiled and nodded. 'I shall look forward to it.' Then she realised something. 'I hope I'm not keeping you from your guests, Mr. Hunter.'

'Not at all,' he assured her. 'But if you are to leave soon, perhaps you would care to dance with me before you go.'

'I would,' Evelyn confirmed, filled with so much excitement she barely knew how to contain it.

Mr. Ashby was dancing happily with his wife. He wished he didn't have to go to Bath on business for he was having a fine time at the ball.

Nearby, Mr. London was still dancing with Primrose. He seemed enthralled with her company and she was obviously flattered by his attention.

Annabel stood aside watching Primrose and Mr. London, unable to shake off the uneasy feeling she had about him.

'Would you care to dance?' a voice said over Annabel's shoulder. She looked, and there was Rupert Feingold smiling pleasantly at her, extending his gloved hand, hoping she'd accept.

Annabel nodded, accepted his hand and let him lead her on to the dance floor. They joined in with the other couples seamlessly. For a moment, they danced beside her parents, all of them smiling at each other as the music played in the background.

Far in the background stood Captain DeGrey. He didn't grudge any of them their happiness, but his heart felt heavy wondering when Evelyn would rejoin the party. He was determined to ask her to dance with him. He hoped she would accept. He was thinking this when he saw Evelyn walk into the ballroom, accompanied by Mr. Hunter, and they immediately joined the dancing.

The disappointment hit him hard. It was as if every chance afforded to him was being stolen away by circumstances beyond his control.

Amid the crowd of guests standing around the ballroom, or dancing, Captain DeGrey felt completely alone. Whatever was about to happen that evening, he had a sinking feeling that dancing with Evelyn would prove elusive. He watched the most distinguished man in the ballroom dancing with the woman he'd long loved. Of all the suitors to be his rival it had to Sabastien Hunter.

'Promise you'll write to me,' Mrs. Ashby insisted as Mr. Ashby got ready to leave in the carriage. The front of Heather Park was still ablaze with torches and people arriving late to the ball. Their carriage was the only one leaving early.

'I will be home before the letter arrives, my dear,' Mr. Ashby told her.

Mrs. Ashby brushed this aside. 'It doesn't matter. I want you to promise to write. You know I like to receive letters.'

'I promise,' he told his wife, and kissed her lovingly on the cheek before leaving.

Annabel and Primrose hugged Evelyn, and giggled from the news she'd relayed quickly about her invitation to paint at Heather Park.

Taking Evelyn's hand, Mr. Ashby helped her into the carriage.

'Look after each other,' Mrs. Ashby said, sounding stressed and almost teary. 'You know I worry about you when you're away, especially in Bath, where there are all sorts of curmudgeons.'

Nodding and waving, the carriage took Evelyn and her father away from the fun of the evening, on a night that Evelyn would've dearly loved to have stayed and danced until the dawn.

Evelyn had her velvet cloak on, but she also put a blanket over her knees, prepared to sleep for most of the journey to Bath. In the distance she saw the lights of Heather Park, and the imposing silhouette of the house. The view faded as the carriage continued on, though the impression Mr. Hunter had instilled in her lingered long into the journey, until she fell asleep while picturing herself dancing with him and all eyes on them.

CHAPTER FOUR

Mrs. Ashby and Annabel watched Primrose dancing with Mr. London.

'Mr. London is a very fine gentleman,' Mrs. Ashby began, and then frowned. 'But I wish that he wouldn't encroach on Primrose's entire evening.'

Mrs. Ashby's voice was so shrill that Captain DeGrey overheard her comment and glanced at Mr. London dancing with Primrose.

'Surely she must find a moment to herself,' Annabel complained.

'Oh, there's Lady Thornbee and Miss Octavia.' Mrs. Ashby looked across the room at them standing talking to some other guests.

Annabel was curious. 'Do you know the couple they're talking to?' She viewed the man, in his twenties, tall and handsome with dark hair, an athletic build and capable demeanour. The woman he was with had dark hair too, the palest of complexions and a beauty that matched his handsomeness.

'I believe that's Mr. Crispin Midwinter,' Mrs. Ashby revealed. 'And his cousin, Miss Charmaine Midwinter.'

'The Midwinters from Blackhall?'

'I believe so.' Mrs. Ashby studied Mr. Midwinter. 'I don't think I've ever seen so many fine and handsome young men at a single ball in my experience.'

'No, indeed,' Annabel agreed.

'Mr. Midwinter is the other gentlemen Lady Thornbee spoke of. He recently inherited Blackhall from his late grandfather,' said Mrs. Ashby.

'So he's the third young gentlemen to move to the neighbourhood?' Annabel enquired.

'He is. Lady Thornbee mentioned that his cousin Charmaine had accompanied him.'

As they were talking, Primrose managed to pry herself away from dancing with Mr. London and walked over to join them.

Mrs. Ashby fanned Primrose as she sighed with mild exhaustion. 'I'm happy you've taken a break from dancing with Mr. London. If Mr. Ashby had still been here, I trust he would've intervened.'

‘Mr. London is very pleasant company,’ said Primrose, ‘but I’d hoped to dance with others as well as him. People will think we’ve formed an attachment and this is not correct.’ She wasn’t ruling out the possibility, but felt too pressured, too quickly.

‘Oh, here he comes again,’ Mrs. Ashby warned them, seeing Mr. London walking towards them after having sipped some refreshment.

Sensing their predicament, Captain DeGrey stepped in and joined their company, giving them a knowing look, as if he understood their predicament.

‘May I have the next dance, Miss Primrose?’ Captain DeGrey said politely.

Relieved to be rescued, Primrose immediately smiled, nodded and took his hand.

Captain DeGrey pretended not to notice Mr. London’s reaction at being thwarted as he walked past him, leading Primrose on to the dance floor.

Instead of joining Mrs. Ashby and Annabel, Mr. London spun around and ventured elsewhere, bristling slightly and glaring over his shoulder at Captain DeGrey.

Mrs. Ashby squeezed Annabel’s hand in relief, but they barely had a moment to view the captain dancing with Primrose, when a man’s voice interrupted.

‘Miss Annabel, would you care to dance with me?’ Mr. Feingold said, smiling at her.

Annabel accepted his invitation and they joined in the dancing.

Happy to see her daughters enjoying the ball, Mrs. Ashby wandered around admiring the splendour. She also saw Lady Thornbee and Octavia talking to Mr. London, and moments later, he escorted Octavia on to the dance floor. Mrs. Ashby was relieved to see him pay attention to Octavia, giving Primrose room to breathe and circulate with other gentlemen, like Captain DeGrey.

‘Thank you, captain,’ said Primrose as they danced.

He knew what she meant and nodded politely. He’d been happy to rescue her from her predicament with Mr. London.

After dancing a little, they stood aside and chatted while Mr. London continued dancing with Octavia Thornbee.

‘Is your sister, Miss Evelyn, viewing the Heather Park art?’ Captain DeGrey said, glancing around, wondering where she was.

'No, Evelyn has left to travel to Bath with my father. He has business there, and my sister is accompanying him.'

The disappointment he tried to disguise was evident.

'Is something wrong, captain? Did you wish to talk to Evelyn about an important matter?' Primrose asked.

He hesitated. 'No...I...' He forced a smile. 'I was hoping to dance with her this evening.' He'd missed his chance yet again. He was angry with himself. He shouldn't have hesitated for one second. He should've asked her to dance the moment they were introduced.

'I'm sure you'll be afforded the opportunity at the next ball,' Primrose told him, and then smiled up at him. 'At Seaforth. I believe you're planning to hold a ball there soon. Or perhaps it's just a rumour.'

'No, it's true. A ball is in the planning,' he confirmed.

'Evelyn will be home soon. The trip to Bath is a short one. She would surely love to attend at Ball at Seaforth, as would I, though I wouldn't presume to be invited.'

'You are indeed invited,' he stated firmly. 'All members of your family are most welcome.'

'I will extend your gracious invitation to my family. They will be delighted. We do so love to dance. And it gives us a legitimate reason for making new dresses,' she said lightly.

He found Primrose to be very pleasant company, and although Evelyn was her sister, he saw little likeness between them. Both were lovely in his eyes, and their manners were most agreeable.

'Miss Evelyn is, I believe, an accomplished artist,' he remarked.

Primrose tilted her head and asked politely. 'Are you acquainted with my sister?'

Was he? He didn't want to lie to Primrose as she was being so sweet, and he hated being dishonest when she was so open.

Primrose waited for his reply, her expression becoming more curious with each second he hesitated.

'I, eh...I remember her from years ago,' he began. 'We never actually spoke, or were introduced, but I saw her several times in town when I was visiting Seaforth while staying with my grandfather.'

'It's a pity you never met her,' Primrose told him.

'It is. She always seemed to be in such happy humour, as did you and Miss Annabel. I remember seeing all of you with your parents.'

'I'm sorry that I don't recall seeing you, captain. I feel we would've been friendly acquaintances, though I suppose you were only a young boy.'

'I was,' he confirmed, 'but the recollections were so pleasant that I have never forgotten them, even though I have been away in the navy for four years.'

'Are you planning to stay long?'

'I'm planning to settle here, if circumstances work out favourably,' he said.

Primrose smiled. 'Then I sincerely hope they do, and you'll have plenty of time to meet Evelyn. She's a very talented artist, and designs all our embroidery patterns.' She held up her bag as an example.

'Very pretty embroidery.'

'My mother and my sisters love to sew and are especially keen to embroider, as am I,' said Primrose.

'Mr. Hunter seemed eager to show your sister the artwork at Heather Park,' he prompted her.

'Yes, we were quite surprised when he invited her to view the art in the drawing room. It's a shame her evening was cut short, but as I say, there will be a ball at Seaforth to look forward to.'

'Indeed.' He nodded, confirming this with her, and convincing himself that his chance with Evelyn would be forthcoming.

'Do you know Mr. Hunter?' she asked him.

'No, I hardly know anyone. People have left or passed, and so much has changed in the years that I've been away.'

'So you won't know Mr. Gilles London either,' she added.

'No, though I assume you do.'

'Not at all. We passed him in town recently, then met him tonight at the ball.'

Captain DeGrey frowned. 'If I may be so bold as to remark — his attention to you was quite intense. I was under the impression that you were long acquainted.'

'I was worried people would think this, and I'm grateful for your intervention.'

He nodded again, assuring her he was fine with this.

'He's dancing with Octavia Thornbee now,' Primrose remarked. 'Octavia is Lady Thornbee's daughter.'

'I am yet to make their acquaintance.' He had noticed Lady Thornbee and her daughter, and assumed them to be social butterflies.

'Mr. Rupert Feingold seems very pleasant,' said Primrose, watching him dancing with Annabel.

'He does. If he's here for the summer, I hope he'll be a guest at my ball.'

'His cousin, Raine Feingold, has invited Evelyn to paint with her at Heather Park upon her return from Bath,' she said. 'It seems we've all made happy new acquaintances during this ball, so I can only hope to extend these at the Seaforth ball.'

'I share your optimism, Miss Primrose.'

She smiled at him in a friendly and genteel manner, and for a moment, just a moment, he noticed how truly beautiful Primrose was. He blinked, and his heart was fully entrenched again in his love for Evelyn, but he could see that it would be easy for any man to adore Primrose Ashby.

The evening continued with people dancing, mingling, being introduced and generally having a great night at the Heather Park ball. Sabastien Hunter was at times elusive, disappearing from the ballroom to other parts of the house, leaving his friend, Rupert Feingold to act as host. It was a task that Mr. Feingold was happy to fulfil, between dancing with Annabel. He danced with her twice, and it would've been a third time if Mr. Crispin Midwinter had not stepped in to ask Annabel to dance with him.

Lady Thornbee had introduced Mr. Midwinter to the Ashby ladies, and as the evening wore on, he finally asked Annabel to dance.

By now Mr. London was dancing with various women, and seemed to have given up on his pursuit of Primrose.

Annabel felt her heart flutter as she danced with Crispin Midwinter. She found Rupert Feingold to be a happy partner, but there was something about Crispin Midwinter that stirred her deepest emotions. He was obviously handsome, but so too were several of the gentlemen she'd danced with. He was quiet, not speaking while they danced which seemed to increase the fluttering in her heart, especially when his eyes, grey, like a stormy sky, looked at her. His dark hair tumbled in ruffled locks over his forehead, emphasising his gaze and fine features. Unlike Mr. Feingold, he didn't have a propensity to smile easily.

He wore gloves, as did everyone, but she felt the strength of his hands holding hers. During the evening she'd heard that Mr. Midwinter was accomplished with a sword and practised his fencing skills at Blackhall. She imagined him, dressed in dark trousers and a white, open neck shirt, crossing swords with his sporting tutor or whoever he sparred with, and her heart thundered at the thought of this.

Annabel scolded herself for letting her thoughts run to such wild imaginings, and concentrated on the present, as Mr. Midwinter led her in the dancing. One dance ended, but he kept a hold of her hand, not in an uncomfortable way, but hesitant to let her go. She made no move to extract herself from his company, and as the next dance began, which was of a very lively nature, she threw herself into the fun and frivolity of it, dancing with this handsome man.

Mr. Feingold was dancing with Primrose, Captain DeGrey was partnered with Miss Raine Feingold, and it was only when the dance was halfway through that Mr. Hunter walked back into the room and stood aside watching his guests delight in the dancing.

Lady Thornbee came over to join Mrs. Ashby. 'Have you seen Mr. London converse at all with Mr. Hunter?'

'No, I have not. If I hadn't been informed that Mr. London was a friend of Mr. Hunter, I wouldn't have taken them to be acquainted in the slightest.'

Lady Thornbee spoke in a confiding tone. 'I agree, and so do a few others I've spoken to.'

'I hope that Mr. London is not some sort of charlatan,' Mrs. Ashby whispered.

'We will soon find out,' Lady Thornbee said, and then headed over to talk to Mr. Hunter.

Mrs. Ashby watched them, and assumed Lady Thornbee had asked him about Mr. London, for there was a reaction from Mr. Hunter that showed his surprise.

'No, I'm not acquainted with Gilles London,' Mr. Hunter said to Lady Thornbee.

Before they could continue, Rupert Feingold came bounding over, full of smiles and enthusiasm. 'Come on, Sabastien, let's have you dancing. You can't be standing here when there are so many young ladies to dance with. It's your ball. Come now.' Not taking no for an answer, Mr. Feingold urged his friend to join in the merriment, and soon the host was part of the dancing, partnered with Primrose, while Mr. Feingold danced with Octavia Thornbee. Her deficit of smiles was outshone by his abundance of cheer.

Lady Thornbee rejoined Mrs. Ashby as they watched the dancing, and connections, unfold.

'Mr. Hunter isn't acquainted with Mr. London,' said Lady Thornbee.

'I saw his reaction,' Mrs. Ashby told her. 'We should be very careful of Mr. London.'

Lady Thornbee nodded, and they continued to view the dancing.

'Mr. Feingold is such a cheerful gentleman, and very good looking too,' Mrs. Ashby remarked.

'Octavia is obviously enjoying his company,' said Lady Thornbee.

Mrs. Ashby kept her opposite opinion to herself, and smiled politely.

By the end of the evening, many new acquaintances had been made, and the atmosphere was bright and lively. Mr. Hunter was repeatedly thanked by his guests for a most welcoming and exhilarating ball, enjoyed by all. Presumably including Octavia Thornbee as she deemed to smile at Mr. Feingold as she was leaving.

Annabel hurried over to her mother with Crispin Midwinter in tow. 'Mr. Midwinter has offered us a ride home in his carriage.'

Mrs. Ashby brightened. 'That's very kind of you, Mr. Midwinter. We would be pleased to accept if it doesn't inconvenience you and Miss Midwinter.'

'Blackhall is on the same route as Heathfield,' Mr. Midwinter assured her. 'And as Mr. Ashby has taken your carriage to Bath, I would be pleased to take you and your daughters home safely.'

With this agreed, Mrs. Ashby, Annabel and Primrose bid good evening to their immediate company, and then thanked Mr. Hunter.

'We've had a wonderful evening,' Mrs. Ashby told him.

'I hope to welcome you back another time, and look forward to Miss Evelyn Ashby joining Miss Feingold for a day of painting at Heather Park.'

'I know that Evelyn is looking forward to it.' Mrs. Ashby smiled and bid Mr. Hunter goodnight, and to the Feingolds standing beside him, and then headed out.

The ball had continued well into the early hours. The dawn was due to rise, creating a beautiful deep blue glow to the sky that arched high above Heather Park. Numerous carriages and horses were being assembled as guests started to leave, and the happy atmosphere that had prevailed inside was continued outside, filling the air with a cheerful ambiance.

As Mr. Midwinter's carriage was brought over, Captain DeGrey came hurrying up to Mrs. Ashby and her daughters.

'May I offer to take you home in my carriage?' he asked them.

Mrs. Ashby smiled at him. 'Thank you, captain, but Mr. Midwinter has been kind enough to offer to take us in his carriage.'

Captain DeGrey smiled tightly, nodded and went to step away when Charmaine Midwinter spoke up. Although introduced at the ball, they had not danced or mingled socially, so her comment took him aback.

'Is it true you're holding a ball at Seaforth soon, captain?' Charmaine asked him outright.

He nodded. 'I would be delighted if you and Mr. Midwinter would be my guests.'

Charmaine smiled at him. 'I shall look forward to it.' She thought how handsome he looked in the torchlight glow, even more so than when he was dancing. Dancing with almost every other lady of her acquaintance, and yet, he hadn't danced with her. If he'd asked her, she would've said yes, but his interest seemed steeped in the Ashby family.

Her smile caught him off guard, and as Mrs. Ashby, Annabel and Primrose were helped into the carriage by Mr. Midwinter, he felt inclined to offer his hand to assist Charmaine into the other seat of the carriage. The look she gave him lingered with him. Her eyes were stunning, but unlike Primrose's pale grey, they were dark grey. Both ladies had heart–shaped faces, but Primrose's lips were fuller and inclined to be smiling. Charmaine's smile was more selective, but perhaps it was a compliment that she bestowed it upon him.

The Ashby ladies sat on one side of the carriage, facing Charmaine and Crispin Midwinter.

Mr. Midwinter noticed Charmaine's interest in the captain, but made no comment.

Captain DeGrey waved as they drove off and walked over to his own carriage, but was waylaid by Rupert Feingold.

'Wasn't that a fine evening,' Mr. Feingold said, sounding elated. 'And a ball at Seaforth now I hear. Not fishing for an invitation of course.'

'I would be happy if you and your cousin, Miss Raine Feingold, would be my guests at the ball. And Mr. Hunter.'

'Thank you. I assume the Ashby family will be in attendance?'

'They will.'

'All of them, including Miss Evelyn Ashby?'

Captain DeGrey nodded. 'I especially hope Miss Evelyn will join us.'

'Wonderful,' Mr. Feingold said, and then bounded off back into the house.

The carriage was brought over for Captain DeGrey, and he stepped in, feeling suddenly all alone as everyone appeared to be leaving with others. He decided to make haste with his plans for the ball at Seaforth. If Primrose was right, and Evelyn was soon to come home from her trip to Bath, a ball would be awaiting her. No mistakes this time.

The chatter in the Midwinter carriage included discussing embroidery as Charmaine Midwinter admired the embroidery work on Annabel and Primrose's dresses and bags.

'I should have brought my sewing box with me to Blackhall,' said Miss Midwinter. 'I love to embroider.'

'We all enjoy sewing and especially like embroidery,' Mrs. Ashby told her.

'I know nothing about embroidery,' Mr. Midwinter confessed. 'But I can appreciate the beauty of it on your dresses.' He smiled particularly at Annabel.

'I think I'll embroider my dress for the Seaforth ball,' said Miss Midwinter, and then she looked at Mrs. Ashby. 'I presume Captain DeGrey is a dear friend of your family.'

'We've actually only been introduced this evening,' Mrs. Ashby revealed.

Miss Midwinter looked surprised. 'But you seem so well acquainted.'

'He remembers us from the past,' Primrose explained. 'We'd never met, but he recalls seeing us in town when he was here visiting his grandfather at Seaforth. He's been away at sea for the past four years. None of us really know him.'

'I believe he has a fine character,' said Mrs. Ashby. 'We would now be pleased to call him an acquaintance.'

Miss Midwinter looked at her cousin. 'You should hold a ball at Blackhall.'

He blinked. 'A ball?'

'Yes,' Miss Midwinter insisted. 'Mr. Hunter held one at Heather Park, Captain DeGrey is holding one at Seaforth, so it's only fitting that you hold one at Blackhall.'

He hesitated. 'I suppose I should...'

'That's settled,' Miss Midwinter was quick to say.

Primrose sounded delighted. 'After Seaforth, we'll have another ball to look forward to.'

'That will be wonderful,' Annabel added, smiling.

Seeing Annabel smile sharpened Crispin Midwinter's resolve to hold at ball at Blackhall. 'I will set plans for it in the morning.'

For the remainder of the carriage ride, the ladies discussed their preferences for dresses and dances for the balls, while Mr. Midwinter nodded, agreeing, taking in the aspects they hoped for.

The carriage pulled up outside Heathfield and Mr. Midwinter jumped out and helped the Ashby ladies from the carriage. Lights shone from inside the house, creating a welcoming glow, as staff awaited their return.

Bidding each other good evening, the carriage drove off, and the Ashby ladies went inside, chatting all the while about the people they'd met, the gossip they'd heard, and got ready for bed.

The dawn was rising by the time everyone was settled.

Annabel lay in bed after blowing out the candle by herself, missing Evelyn, but looking forward to telling her everything that had happened and was going to happen.

Gazing out the window, she hoped Evelyn was safe on her trip to Bath. Perhaps she'd meet someone there that knew Mr. Gilles London. Then she pushed the thought of him aside, and smiled as she recalled dancing with the dashing Crispin Midwinter. Was he interested in her? She dare not get her hopes up, but there was definitely an attraction on her part. Charmaine Midwinter was more difficult to decipher. Her first impression of her was that of a standoffish nature. Perhaps she was shy? But then she reconsidered. Miss Midwinter had surprised even Captain DeGrey with her boldness in asking him if he was having a ball at Seaforth.

Annabel sighed, happy, elated and yet so tired. Sleep stole away the chance to unravel the questions running through her mind.

CHAPTER FIVE

Blackhall dominated the estate. It was a large mansion, dark in manner, set within acres of lush countryside. A thick bank of trees guarded the mansion's back, standing tall, at attention, dark silhouettes against the sky.

It was bordered by beautiful flower gardens, blackthorn hedges, and black poplar trees that gave an impression of elegance. A lake reflected the morning sunlight.

Crispin Midwinter and Charmaine sat in the dining room having breakfast the morning after the Heather Park ball.

'Are you going to keep your promise?' Charmaine asked him, helping herself to a fresh baked scone.

Crispin was tucking into his bread and butter, eggs and cold meat. He paused and nodded. 'I am. Why? Have you changed your mind about wanting a ball here?'

'No, on the contrary. I've been dreaming about it.'

'Dreaming only about the ball, or a particular gentleman that may attend it?' he asked, teasing her.

'I know you're teasing me, but I won't allow you to make me blush,' she told him firmly.

'I doubt I could make you blush even if that was my intention.'

'Perhaps I could make you blush? Though you'd try hide your reaction.'

'You seem confident, so...' he gestured for her to go ahead.

'What about you flirting with Miss Annabel Ashby last night?'

He reacted, and she laughed.

'You may laugh, Charmaine, but I have no intention of pursuing Miss Annabel.'

'You're a poor liar,' she told him, causing him to attempt disinterest in the matter.

'I met a few pleasant young ladies last night, Miss Annabel included, but no one of special interest.'

Charmaine sipped her tea and smiled at him over the rim of her cup.

'I'm serious,' he insisted.

'You're trying to be, but I'm not at all fooled.'

'What about Domenic DeGrey?' he asked.

She put her cup down slowly and sighed. 'I find him...intriguing.'

'Intriguing? Now I am intrigued as to why you think this.'

Charmaine shrugged. 'I suspect he has a deep secret, something he hasn't told anyone.'

'What type of secret?'

'Nothing ominous,' she was quick to say. 'Something of the heart. And there's a sadness to him.'

'You've certainly made him your study. Perhaps you're the one with the secret of the heart, Charmaine.'

She smiled coyly. 'If so, I'll never tell you. At least, not yet.'

'If your intention is to intrigue me, you have succeeded.'

'Good. Life would be so boring without guile and gossip.'

'What gossip have you heard that I should know about?' he asked her.

'Interesting gossip, but you definitely shouldn't know about it,' she told him, and then continued to eat her breakfast.

Smiling at each other, their teasing ended, for the moment, while they sat having breakfast and planning their day.

Charmaine had a request, and a plan for her day, but she needed him to assist her. He seemed in a light mood, and she had an incentive she knew he could not resist.

Mrs. Ashby, Annabel and Primrose sat around the table enjoying breakfast and reliving the fun of the previous night's ball.

'I knew this was going to be an exciting summer season,' Mrs. Ashby trilled. 'Wasn't Mr. Rupert Feingold a delight. And I was so pleased when Captain DeGrey stepped in to save you from dancing to distraction with Mr. London.' She spread raspberry jam on her slice of bread and butter and shook her head in disapproval. 'He's a very devious gentleman.'

'What have you heard?' Primrose said eagerly, cupping her tea.

'Last night, Lady Thornbee asked Sabastien Hunter if he was friends with Mr. London, and he told her he didn't even know him.'

Annabel blinked. 'Really? He said that?'

'Yes. I saw her ask him, and I saw his reaction. If Mr. London is trying to pass himself off as Mr. Hunter's friend, then he's lying. Which we're sure he is.'

'That is so devious,' Primrose said, shuddering at the thought that she'd been dancing with him. 'I certainly won't be dancing with him again.'

'What a charlatan.' Annabel helped herself to another slice of fruit cake.

'I'll be informing Mr. Ashby of everything that happened.' Mrs. Ashby tugged her shawl around her shoulders and looked quite miffed. 'To think that I allowed you to dance with him, Primrose. How dare he act like that in public.' She took a deep, calming breath. 'However, I refuse to let him affect our happiness. We had a wonderful evening, and met lots of very pleasant people.'

'Do you think Mr. Midwinter will keep his word, and plan a ball at Blackhall?' said Annabel.

'I trust he will,' Mrs. Ashby stated. 'He was quite the gentleman to let us ride home in his carriage. And he seemed enamoured with you.' She smiled at Annabel.

Annabel blushed as bright as the raspberry jam they were eating.

Primrose giggled. 'You like him, don't you?'

Annabel concentrated on the food on her plate as she replied. 'Perhaps.'

'Oh! She does like him.' Mrs. Ashby sounded thrilled.

'Mama!' Annabel scolded her. 'I barely know Mr. Midwinter.'

'But that's the fun of romance,' Mrs. Ashby told her. 'Getting to know him.'

Primrose and her mother exchanged delighted smiles.

Annabel turned the attention to Primrose. 'What about you and Captain DeGrey? You were chatting for a while after dancing with him. He seemed disappointed that we were sharing a carriage with Mr. Midwinter, and he was too late with his offer to take us home.'

Primrose gave an honest answer. 'I'm not sure. I thought several gentlemen last night were very nice, including the captain, but I'm not convinced he's interested in me. He spoke quite a bit about Evelyn.'

'Evelyn?' Mrs. Ashby sounded surprised.

'Yes,' said Primrose. 'He seemed disconcerted to find out that she'd left the ball and gone to Bath. He said he'd wanted to dance with her.'

Mrs. Ashby and Annabel were taken aback.

Primrose continued. 'When he spoke about Evelyn, there was something in his manner that was intense.'

'He only met her recently,' Annabel said, recalling their encounter when she was out walking. 'His horse almost trampled her. Then he met her at the ball. He didn't dance with her.'

'But he wanted to,' Primrose reminded them. 'However, Mr. Hunter swept her away to see the paintings.'

Mrs. Ashby started to review her opinion. 'So he did. Now that I think about it, he appeared to be quite disappointed.'

Annabel sounded protective of her sister. 'I hope the captain wasn't just dancing with you to glean information about Evelyn.'

'No, I don't think that for a moment,' Primrose insisted. 'His intention was to help me out of my predicament with Gilles London. He was quite genuine. He's not underhanded like Mr. London.'

They all agreed on this.

'Perhaps Evelyn will enlighten us when she comes home,' said Mrs. Ashby. 'Maybe she knows something about Captain DeGrey.'

Annabel shook her head. 'Evelyn would've told me if she did.'

'Well, I'm sure we'll find out soon,' Mrs. Ashby assured her.

They continued to have a leisurely breakfast, having slept later than usual. But there was no hurry to their day, or particular plans.

While they were still having breakfast and chatting, Tilsy came hurrying in to Mrs. Ashby.

'Excuse me, ma'am, but a carriage has arrived with Mr. Midwinter and Miss Midwinter. They've requested to call on you.'

A flurry of activity disturbed their relaxed morning. Mrs. Ashby jumped up and hurried her daughters through to the parlour.

'Hurry up, girls,' she said in an urgent whisper.

They ran through to the parlour and picked up their embroidery, while Mrs. Ashby lifted a book from a shelf and they all sat down, feigning calm.

'Show them in, Tilsy.'

Moments later Tilsy brought the two guests in, and the Ashby ladies stood up to greet them.

'I hope we're not disturbing you,' said Mr. Midwinter.

Mrs. Ashby smiled in welcome. 'No, do come in. Can I offer you some tea?'

'We weren't planning to interrupt,' Miss Midwinter explained. 'I persuaded my cousin to go with me into town to buy items so that I may embroider. But I wondered if you could recommend any particular shops that we should visit.'

Annabel was the first to reply. 'Yes, the liner draper's shop is excellent. It has a fine stock of fabric and thread.'

Mrs. Ashby had a suggestion. 'But we have plenty of fabric and thread that we'd be happy to share with you.'

'Oh, I couldn't impose,' Miss Midwinter said, while hoping she could.

Primrose opened her sewing box. 'I have pieces of white linen that are perfect for embroidery work.' She lifted them out and showed Charmaine.

'Or you can help yourself to thread if you have items at Blackhall you'd prefer to embroider — a dress, table linen...'

'I'd love to embroider the neckline of a couple of dresses, but I don't have any patterns or thread, and I'm a bit out of practise and nowhere near your level of skill.' She gazed around and admired the framed embroideries. 'These are so lovely.'

'Come and join us anytime and we'll be happy to give you patterns and teach you any stitches you like,' said Mrs. Ashby.

Miss Midwinter was delighted. 'Are you sure?'

'Yes,' Mrs. Ashby confirmed. 'While you're staying at Blackhall, join us for sewing. We're always sewing, aren't we girls?'

Annabel and Primrose nodded, both happy to have Miss Midwinter join in their company.

Amid the excited chatter of the ladies, Crispin Midwinter stood tall, admiring the homeliness, the artistic element of the framed embroideries and watercolour paintings. He liked what he saw. He liked that they were happy to make Charmaine welcome. And he liked seeing Annabel again. She looked lovely, fresh faced, in a pale blue dress, with her hair tumbling around her shoulders and pinned up at the sides. At the ball, he'd been transfixed by her beauty, but if the truth be known, her beauty was even finer with less enhancement. Caught in her natural morning appearance, Annabel was a true beauty. As was Primrose. But it was Annabel who had disturbed this dreams the previous night. And when Charmaine suggested they pay the Ashby family a visit, he'd heartily agreed.

Tilsy brought tea and cake into the parlour, and the two guests were seated. All consideration of heading into town was brushed aside in favour of enjoying the morning where they were.

If Mr. Midwinter was at all bored with their sewing chatter, he hid it well. But he wasn't bored, he was exactly where he would've wanted to be that morning — in the company of Annabel Ashby.

Evelyn breathed in the morning air in Bath as she stepped from the carriage and headed into the house. It was situated in one of the prestigious crescents in the heart of the town. A bright, clear blue sky arched overhead, and the promise of a lovely summer's day was assured.

Mr. Ashby led the way in to the front entrance. They were staying with her father's brother and his wife. They were affluent and enjoyed a busy social life.

Evelyn was very fond of her aunt and uncle. She hadn't seen them for over a year, and was looking forward to spending time with them during her short stay in Bath.

The welcome was as warm as ever, and although her father had to attend to business, Evelyn was swept into her aunt and uncle's world that began with a trip round the best shops in Bath. Her aunt was the sweetest of characters, and her uncle had such a good nature that spending time with them always resulted in Evelyn feeling lighter in spirit. So that evening when they'd been invited along to a social event, she'd been happy to go with them. Dancing and socialising aplenty was enjoyed by Evelyn, and the supper had such fine food.

Evelyn's father was attending a business supper, so she went to the assembly without him.

It was during the evening while dancing, that Evelyn was taken aback to see Mr. Sabastien Hunter join the company. He arrived quite late, but as the evening extended into the late hours, there was plenty of time for Mr. Hunter to enjoy the party.

'Oh, there's Mr. Sabastien Hunter,' Evelyn whispered to her aunt, seeing him standing on the opposite side of the room having just arrived.

Her aunt glanced over at the gentleman she'd indicated. 'Do you know him?'

Evelyn explained about the ball at Heather Park.

Her aunt was interested in every aspect.

'He didn't mention that he was coming to Bath,' Evelyn confided. 'Even though I told him I was travelling here with my father.'

'Perhaps he's looking for you, my dear,' her aunt suggested.

Evelyn's heart jolted at the thought that this could be true. Had Mr. Hunter come here to pursue her?

'What are you two mischief makers whispering about?' Evelyn's uncle asked them, joining them after having some refreshments.

'That gentleman over there knows Evelyn,' his wife said, pointing across with her fan. 'It would be so romantic if he was here in pursuit of our niece.'

'It would indeed,' he agreed.

Evelyn wasn't sure what to do, but the decision was taken away from her the moment Mr. Hunter saw her and came striding over.

Mr. Hunter bowed politely. 'Miss Ashby.'

Evelyn nodded acknowledgment. 'Mr. Hunter. This is my aunt and uncle. My father isn't here this evening. He's dealing with business elsewhere in Bath.'

With the pleasantries of introductions made, there was a tension as Sabastien Hunter hesitated, wondering what to do.

'Are you here on business, Mr. Hunter?' her aunt asked.

'Yes, and no,' he replied ambiguously.

Evelyn frowned. 'Is it a secret?' she asked lightly, not expecting the answer she received from him.

'It is.' Mr. Hunter's tone left no room for teasing.

'I trust that you are fit to deal with it,' her uncle said to him.

'I am, but I would ask for your assistance in this matter as it affects Miss Ashby,' Mr. Hunter explained.

'Affects me? In what way, sir?' Evelyn asked him.

'Regarding Mr. Gilles London,' Mr. Hunter told her.

At the mention of his name, her aunt and uncle exchanged a knowing glance.

Mr. Hunter picked up on this. 'Do you know Mr. London?'

'We know of him,' said her aunt.

'Gilles London has a bit of a reputation in Bath,' her uncle confided.

'What sort of reputation?' asked Mr. Hunter.

'Nothing untoward in a financial or business sense,' her uncle elaborated. 'He's rich, from a wealthy family, so money is not a cause for concern. He flatters and cajoles his way into the hearts of pretty young ladies. Not to steal their fortunes, but to take advantage of their favours.'

Evelyn frowned. 'Favours?'

Her aunt gave her a nudge. 'You know. Lavishing romantic attention on naive young women in society, and then discarding them once his...pleasures are spent, shall we say.' She gave a disapproving look.

'So he's a philanderer,' Mr. Hunter said, having his suspicions confirmed.

Evelyn's uncle nodded. 'It's no secret in Bath. Mr. London is one of several young gentlemen of fortune with questionable morals.'

'Gilles London is not the type of acquaintance any young lady should have anything to do with, especially if she wants to keep her reputation unsullied,' her aunt warned them.

'Do you have reason to suspect his misbehaviour?' her uncle asked Mr. Hunter.

'I do. He attended my Heather Park ball last night, and a few trusted friends expressed their concern about his reasons for being there. I do not recall inviting him. He told people he was a friend of mine, yet I had never met him until the ball.'

'His sort have a tendency to do that,' her uncle said.

'Mr. London paid particular attention to Primrose,' said Evelyn. 'After I left, did he continue to dance repeatedly with her?' she asked Mr. Hunter.

'He did, but then Captain Domenic DeGrey intervened,' Mr. Hunter explained. 'Your mother and Miss Annabel were most grateful for his assistance. Mr. London then seemed to flit around like a butterfly, dancing with numerous young ladies.'

'Such shocking behaviour,' Evelyn complained.

'If I had known his character, I would not have allowed him to do this,' Mr. Hunter assured her.

Evelyn nodded, accepting this as true. 'So that's why you're here in Bath, to find out about him?'

'Mainly,' Mr. Hunter replied, 'but I hoped to perhaps see you while I was in Bath.'

Evelyn blushed at his forthright reply. 'Oh.'

The attraction between Evelyn and Sabastien Hunter was palpable.

Evelyn's uncle smiled at his wife. 'I was about to ask you to dance, my dear.' He held out his hand and she smiled as she accepted it.

'It was delightful to meet you, Mr. Hunter,' said her aunt. 'I'm sure we'll have time to chat later, but I do so like to dance.'

Part excuse, part truth, her aunt and uncle headed on to the dance floor leaving Evelyn in the company of Mr. Hunter.

'Is my sister, Primrose, aware of Mr. London's dubious character?' Evelyn asked him.

He shook his head. 'Not in such detail, but I believe your mother and Miss Annabel were astute enough to feel suspicious of his undivided attention on Primrose. They properly dealt with this. With the help of Captain DeGrey.'

'Did Mr. London dance with Annabel?'

'Not to my knowledge.'

Evelyn sighed. 'Thank goodness, but what a devious sort of man he is. We believed him to be a friend of yours.'

'No, he's not.'

'Surely he knew he'd be caught out.'

'Perhaps his confidence overruled his common sense,' Mr. Hunter suggested.

Evelyn nodded. 'An arrogant man is often foiled by his own sense of importance.'

'I apologise for having allowed Mr. London to conduct himself recklessly at Heather Park.'

'I do not blame you, sir. The fault lies solely with Mr. London.'

Feeling that the matter was settled somewhat, he invited her to dance. 'Would you care to dance with me this evening?'

'I would,' she said.

For the next few dances, Evelyn and Sabastien were happy together, as if the hours since they'd last danced together at Heather Park had folded seamlessly into the evening in Bath.

CHAPTER SIX

As the evening event drew to a close, Evelyn and Sabastien Hunter stood outside the main room on the balcony, breathing in the calm night air, and gazing out at the view of Bath.

'It's beautiful,' Evelyn said, sighing. 'But my home will always be in the country, at Heathfield.'

While she continued to admire the view, he gazed longingly at her. 'Very beautiful,' he said softly.

The gentleness of his voice made her look at him, such a contrast to the strong, deep voice that made her heart flutter. The sense of being near him made her feel excited. His soft tone made her realise that his feelings for her were perhaps in tune with her own. There was definitely a connection between them.

'Miss Ashby, I was wondering if you'd like to accompany me tomorrow for a walk around Bath. Enjoy the benefits of the water, take in the splendour of Bath. Bring your aunt and uncle of course, and your father if he's available.'

'I would love to, thank you. I shall ask my aunt and uncle, but unfortunately I know that my father will still be dealing with his business meetings.'

At that moment, Evelyn's aunt and uncle wandered out to the balcony in search of her, and she told them of Mr. Hunter's invitation, which they were delighted to accept. He arranged to call on them at their house after breakfast the following day.

Mr. Hunter bid them all good night. 'Until tomorrow then.' Smiling again at Evelyn, he left her in their company.

Evelyn's aunt smiled at her. 'Mr. Hunter is very taken with you, my dear.'

'Indeed he is,' her uncle agreed.

Evelyn couldn't contain the blush forming across her cheeks. 'I find his company most pleasant and enlightening.'

Her aunt and uncle did not tease her any further, and after bidding good night to some of their friends, they headed home in their carriage.

Evelyn looked out the window of the carriage as it travelled through the heart of Bath. The sights and sounds of the city, bustling with social activity, were in such contrast to the quietude of her home in the countryside. The social calendar of her aunt and uncle was filled with invitations to attend balls, assemblies, concerts and all sorts of popular activities.

The street lamps created a glow to the houses and fashionable shops. Bath thrived on being a fashion hub, and Evelyn was looking forward to visiting the shops.

As the carriage pulled up outside her aunt and uncle's house, so too did her father's carriage. They all went inside, exchanging gossip and news of their plans for the following day, then got ready for bed.

Evelyn was pleased to hear that her father's business dealings were prosperous, and that the trip to Bath had been worthwhile. He had other business meetings to deal with, but was happy that they were planning a day with Sabastien Hunter. And as promised to his wife, he wrote another letter to Mrs. Ashby, assuring her that all was well, that he missed her dearly, and would be home soon.

Evelyn pleated her long hair as she gazed out her bedroom window at the city. Wearing her cotton nightdress, she then climbed into bed, blew out the candle, and fell asleep thinking about Sabastien Hunter.

Before retiring for the night, Sabastien wrote an urgent letter to his friend, Rupert Feingold, warning him of the dubious character of Gilles London. In the message he advised that this information was to be used to prevent Mr. London from further devious intentions, particularly upon unsuspecting young ladies in the Heather Park neighbourhood. He trusted that Rupert would use discretion in this matter. Folding the sheet of paper on which the message was written with ink and quill, he addressed it, sealed it with red wax, and dispatched it immediately.

Mr. Hunter was staying in upmarket accommodation in Bath, not far from Evelyn's aunt and uncle's house. Having dealt with the letter, he got undressed, put on a nightshirt and went to bed.

His thoughts drifted to Evelyn Ashby. Her beauty, her manner and her company were everything he desired in a wife, though marriage hadn't been a priority when he'd inherited Heather Park. Quite the opposite. He'd planned to settle into his new life there, while also planning to make frequent trips to London. The city suited him. He thrived there, and had never yearned for the slower pace of life in the countryside. However, the inheritance was of an appealing nature, and he greatly admired the splendour of the house and estate. But he wondered if he'd miss his life in London, and if so, he aimed to split his time unevenly between the two. The preference would be given to London, his home, the only place he'd ever lived, until the inheritance of a countryside residence. Marriage had never been foremost in his mind, though in the past two or three years when he'd seen friends and acquaintances marry, he knew one day he'd be inclined to find a suitable partner. There was one stipulation. He would only ever marry for love, or not at all. He'd never been in love, or felt as strongly and engagingly as he did towards Miss Ashby. The feeling was so heady, a sense of elation and excitement, the moment he first saw her. He loved to read, and in many books he'd read descriptions of romantic love amid some great adventurous story. And now, he was experiencing those feelings himself. Gallantry mattered to him, it always had, and he would never dream of standing back while a woman was in danger or distress when his intervention would protect her. Yet, the strong need and want to protect Evelyn Ashby far exceeded this. Everything in him wanted to protect and provide for her. If this was what falling in love felt like, he was surely smitten.

The thought of Gilles London using his false smiles and fake chivalry to worm his way into Miss Ashby's affections made his blood run wild.

Taking a calming breath, he took comfort in knowing that the truth about the underhanded charlatan was on its speedy way to Heather Park on an overnight carriage. In the morning, the letter would be delivered to Rupert.

He would not trouble Miss Ashby or her relatives in Bath with what he'd done. The matter would be dealt with properly and without fuss.

Thankfully, the thought of Miss Ashby, as lovely as she was dancing with him earlier in the evening, calmed his riled senses in regards to Gilles London. The stirring of his blood and thundering heart was caused only by his longing for her.

The walk round Bath the following morning was invigorating, as was the company. Evelyn and her aunt were escorted by Sabastien Hunter to partake of the water tasting in Bath, and then strolled around the shops. Evelyn's uncle was at a business meeting with her father, something that had already been planned. Aunt Ashby had intended taking Evelyn shopping, so the only change had been the excursion to drink the water, and the pleasant company of Mr. Hunter.

He had assured them that his carriage was on hand should either of the ladies wish to take a rest from walking, but Evelyn loved walking in the countryside and window shopping around Bath was a delight for her. Aunt Ashby was of a similar mind. Pleased to have her niece visiting, she planned to thoroughly spoil her by taking her to shops she knew she'd like and buy her gifts of fabric from the linen drapers and items from the haberdashery.

Evelyn looked at the wonderful window display. The haberdashery had a great selection of bonnets, fans, parasols and gloves as well as exquisite fabric and trimmings. She couldn't wait to take a look inside, though she was aware that this shop might not interest Mr. Hunter.

'I'm interested in whatever you're interested in,' Mr. Hunter assured Evelyn.

Delighted, Evelyn and her aunt ventured inside accompanied by Mr. Hunter.

'I'd like to find items to take home to my sisters and my mother,' Evelyn told them. Her father had given her an allowance to cover such costs, but her aunt would not hear of her spending her money.

'No, Evelyn,' Aunt Ashby insisted. 'This is my treat. I have so few chances to spoil my niece,' she added, smiling at Mr. Hunter.

'I would like to spoil both of you,' he said, but again, Aunt Ashby wouldn't let him pay for anything. As well as wanting to buy gifts for Evelyn personally, she didn't want her niece to be in any way beholden to Mr. Hunter, even though he was an excellent companion for their trip out in Bath.

Understanding that Aunt Ashby was dealing with this, they continued to browse the shop, picking up items of interest.

'Primrose would love these artificial flowers for her hats and bonnets,' Evelyn said, selecting sprigs of blue forget–me–not flowers, pretty daisies and lily of the valley flowers.

Her aunt added a few extra choices including orange blossom and pink and white gypsophila. 'Share these with Annabel and your mother. And what flowers would you like, Evelyn?'

'Bluebells and those blue daisies. I've never seen such pretty flowers.' Evelyn pictured adding these to her hats or pinning a sprig on one of her reticules.

These were added to the purchases along with lots of ribbons and trims to match in blue, pink, yellow and lilac colours. Evelyn selected lace trim she knew her mother would love.

Aunt Ashby lifted a lovely bonnet down from a shelf and insisted Evelyn should have it.

'Thank you, it's lovely,' Evelyn said to her aunt.

'This shop is quite beautiful,' Mr. Hunter said, looking around, interested in the array of coloured fabrics and accessories on display. The floor to ceiling shelves were stacked with all sorts of pretty things. He lifted down a parasol and asked for their opinion. 'Do you think my friend Rupert's cousin, Raine Feingold, would like something like this? I feel she should benefit from a small gift from Bath.'

Evelyn and Aunt Ashby nodded.

'Oh, yes,' said Evelyn. 'Any young lady would delight in such a gift.'

'Good,' he said and proceeded to purchase it while Evelyn chose more fabric for sewing dresses.

'Mr. Hunter is very thoughtful,' Aunt Ashby whispered to Evelyn. 'What a lovely gesture to take something home for his friend's cousin.'

Evelyn whispered back. 'Miss Feingold will appreciate it.' She went on to explain that they were going to paint together at Heather Park.

'I'm pleased you've made a new friend in Raine Feingold.'

Mr. Hunter had paid for the parasol and overheard their conversation as he wandered back to join them. 'If you're ever visiting the Ashby family at Heathfield, I do hope you and your husband will also visit me at Heather Park.'

Aunt Ashby was taken back by the invitation, and more than happy to accept. 'Thank you. We would love to visit you.'

With their purchases paid for, they left the shop. Mr. Hunter carried the bags of items and put them for safe keeping in his carriage, then they continued to stroll and window shop while the sun burned bright in the midday sky.

They visited a bookshop where Mr. Hunter bought a couple of books, and then they stopped for tea, cake and ice cream at a tea shop.

Later at a confectioners, they sampled candied fruits and butterscotch.

During their light conversations, no mention was made regarding Gilles London. Instead, they learned a little more about their simple pleasures, of walking, enjoying pleasant company, reading, art and painting, and dancing. Evelyn learned that Mr. Hunter was an avid attendant of social events in London, including concerts and balls, but he also liked to stroll around the parks and visit the galleries on occasion. He loved reading and had a library of favourite books that he'd yet to transfer to Heather Park. His house in London was still a residence he planned to keep for his frequent visits to the city, and staff were there looking after everything while he lived at Heather Park.

'I could of course stay in a hotel during my London trips,' he explained to them, 'but I see no benefit in giving up my townhouse.'

Financially, he could easily afford to keep both, and for the time being, that's what he was doing.

'My husband is more familiar with London that I am,' said Aunt Ashby. 'I was born and raised in Bath. Are you familiar with Bath?' she asked him.

'Not particularly,' he replied. 'I have visited several times, but my life has tended to be in London or Heather Park, mainly the former.'

'This is only my second trip to Bath,' Evelyn told him. 'I've been to London only once and found it enthralling.'

'Should you wish to visit London, I would be happy to make my townhouse and staff available during your trip,' he said to them.

Both Evelyn and her aunt were grateful for such an offer.

As the day wore on, they took the carriage back to Aunt Ashby's house, where Mr. Hunter bid them good day. But before he left, a further invitation to attend a social event that evening was extended to him by Aunt Ashby, and he was pleased to accept.

Evelyn hadn't known about the invitation, and it was no exaggeration to say that her aunt and uncle had an enviably busy social life in Bath. They seemed to thrive on it, and yet Evelyn thought that she would require equal amounts of quiet evenings sewing or painting. And she would dearly miss her walks in the country and the sea near Heathfield.

That night, Evelyn wore a dress loaned to her by her aunt. It was a new dress and the height of fashion. They were of similar height and slender build, and so the fit was ideal.

Evelyn admired the palest lilac dress fabric, loving the silky beauty of it.

'The dress suits you far better than me,' her aunt said, fussing over her, and then standing back to admire her niece. 'I have gloves and a bag that will be perfect with this dress.'

Aunt Ashby picked out the gloves from a dressing table in the bedroom, and the small evening bag from a cupboard. She handed them to Evelyn.

'You're so kind,' Evelyn said, smiling at her.

'I'm just happy to have you here. What a fun evening we'll have.'

And they did. There was dancing and a dinner was served.

Evelyn's father was there, and she enjoyed dancing with a few partners including Mr. Hunter.

The hosts were friends of Evelyn's aunt and uncle, and were pleased that Evelyn and her father had joined their company. It was indeed a fun evening, with most of the guests taking part in the dancing.

During one of the dances when Evelyn was partnered with Mr. Hunter, a friend of his waved over to him, and when they finished dancing, the man approached them, smiling, delighted to see Mr. Hunter and eager to meet the young lady he was partnered with. The man looked young and affluent.

'Hunter!' the man said, beaming at him, 'what are you doing in Bath?'

'I'm here on business and personal matters,' Mr. Hunter explained politely. Then he introduced Evelyn to the man, and they continued their conversation.

'I thought you'd be at Heather Park. How is the country life suiting you? Missing London yet?' the man asked.

'The country is a lot quieter, but it suits me quite well. But I think I shall always miss London.'

Evelyn's heart jolted in disappointment. Hearing Mr. Hunter say that the country suited him only quite well, made her wonder if he'd ever really settle there, especially as he seemed set to permanently miss London. Such feelings would surely make living at Heather Park less settled. This realisation unsettled her.

'I'm going for a jaunt around Bath in the morning if you'd care to join me,' the man offered.

'Thank you, but I'm travelling to London in the morning. This was just a short trip to Bath.'

The man nodded and then smiled at Evelyn. 'It was a pleasure to make your acquaintance. I hope to meet you and Hunter again soon, in London.' He was then swept into the festivities, leaving Evelyn feeling as if her hopes had been swept away.

She looked at Mr. Hunter, but his expression showed no depths of dismay. He smiled and seemed unaware of her emotional disruption. She allowed herself to be led into the dancing again, but all the while she kept thinking how wrong her assumptions were. But of course, it made sense. A man like Sabastien Hunter wouldn't easily leave the city behind to settle into a quiet country life. It would take time and adjustment to forgo the busy fanfare of concerts and a society that revolved around the heart of London. Whatever pleasures she treasured from living at Heathfield, and no matter the loveliness of the countryside in every season, this was what her heart loved, not his. By inheriting a country estate he was now responsible for its smooth running and upkeep, but this she was certain he could handle easily as his wealth ensured it. But giving up everything he'd ever loved in London, and still clearly adored, would not be so easy.

As the dance finished she was still deep in thought, and he mistook her frown for fatigue.

'Shall we step aside and sit down for tea?' he suggested.

She nodded and let him lead her over to one of the tables where they were served tea and biscuits. She continued to be quiet. He hadn't even mentioned to her that he was due to leave Bath in the morning. Not that it would've altered their day shopping, but she would have preferred to have known that this was his last night in Bath.

'How much longer is your father here on business?' he asked her.

'Only a few days, so we will be going home soon.'

'I have enjoyed our time together, and hope that I may continue to see you when you get home.'

'Yes,' she heard herself say, while her heart was filled with doubt. It would be so easy to fall in love with Sabastien Hunter, and perhaps she had already fallen a little. But the depths of disappointment from an unsettled attachment made her too wary to let her heart be fooled into thinking there was a permanence to their friendship.

Soon they were joined by her family members, and the gaps in her conversation that she now felt with Mr. Hunter were filled with chatter and laughter. Their smiles brightened her thoughts.

The remainder of the night was cheerful, and when it was time to bid farewell to Mr. Hunter as their carriages awaited to head in different directions, Evelyn sensed that perhaps things would be different now. If she had to decide on a happy life, she would stand firm in her love for the country. The city was fine, but she found Bath to be so busy and bustling with activity. London, she remembered, was even more crowded. In a perfect world she could have both quiet times and lively company. But both of these she already had living at Heathfield. London could never offer her both.

Their parting that evening was tinged with sadness, mainly due to Evelyn's realisation that things between her and Sabastien were not to be as straightforward as she'd wished. She stood alongside her family members and waved him goodbye as he was driven off in his carriage. His mood was that of anticipation, looking forward to seeing Evelyn again when he went back to Heather Park.

'Are you all right, my dear?' her aunt asked her quietly as their own carriage drove up to collect them.

'Yes, I am quite well,' Evelyn said in a voice that sounded unsteady. Brushing away a giveaway tear so that no one noticed her unhappiness, she forced a smile and alighted into the carriage. It drove off in the opposite direction, and she couldn't help feeling that this was a slight parting of the ways for her and Sabastien Hunter. Time would tell if her senses were fooling her.

During the next few days, Evelyn took comfort in her aunt's cheerful company, going shopping, visiting an art gallery, taking the waters again at Bath, and attending various social events each evening. Her father and her uncle had joined them for the evening parties and assemblies. The warmth of her family members and the pleasant company of the party hosts and guests helped her not to dwell on disappointed thoughts of Sabastien Hunter.

CHAPTER SEVEN

The warning letter from Sabastien Hunter had felt like a ton weight on Rupert Feingold's shoulders, but he bore the responsibility without complaint. Throughout the days since the news arrived he'd set about informing those people most likely to be affected by Gilles London's disreputable character. This included Crispin Midwinter.

Rupert Feingold had been particularly eager to inform Mr. Midwinter because he'd heard that Mr. London had shown a recent but intense interest in Charmaine Midwinter. Apparently, Miss Midwinter had been sewing daily with Mrs. Ashby and her daughters at Heathfield while Evelyn was in Bath, and Mr. London had called upon the Ashby household with the aim of seeing Miss Primrose. However, on finding out that Charmaine Midwinter was there, he'd set his attentions on her. Flattered, she'd invited him to take tea with her and her cousin at Blackhall, an offer he'd gladly accepted. He'd extended his visit to dining with them, and repeated this the following day, flattering Miss Midwinter with his undivided attention, and ingratiating himself with her cousin. He'd made his intentions clear that he wished to form an attachment to Miss Midwinter. Although she hadn't decided on her feelings towards him, apart from the effects of flattery from such a handsome and affluent man, her heart was being persuaded to trust him. Her actions were sincere. His were not.

Rupert Feingold went personally to Blackhall to talk to Crispin Midwinter. On finding out about Gilles London's devious behaviour, Mr. Midwinter challenged Mr. London to a duel. Swords were their chosen weapon.

Miss Midwinter had tried to halt the combat, not wishing anyone to be hurt on her behalf, but Mr. Midwinter would not be deterred. It was a matter of honour. They would settle the offence like gentlemen. In truth, he had to hold his temper and not start a common fist fight right there and then.

Gilles London appeared, on the surface, to be a gentleman of unadventurous character, but it transpired that his upbringing had included riding and swordsmanship, both things he was skilled at.

Crispin Midwinter was highly trained in all sorts of outdoor activities, and was skilled at fencing. But Mr. London's threat to her cousin sent chills through Charmaine.

'You will lose,' Gilles London told him before storming away.

Crispin Midwinter had heard many a threat or show of confidence from other rivals or competitors, but although he didn't admit it to Charmaine, he shared the chill she felt.

The master swordsman he'd trained under had always told him never to underestimate an opponent. Never. And so when the dawn was due to break over the edge of the lake at Blackhall where their clash was to take place, he was determined to stay rapier sharp and not underrate Gilles London's capability.

The calm mist filtering over the lakeside subdued some of the anger Crispin Midwinter felt towards Gilles London. But seeing his confident smirk, and thinking of his fake smiles and attention to Charmaine, this lit a fire under his determination to deal with the scoundrel. He had no intention of killing him, but he would cut him deep, a reminder never to dare interfere with her emotions again, or ruin her trust in others due to his lies.

Mr. Midwinter wore a white shirt, open at the neck, with a stylish waistcoat and dark trousers tucked into long boots. His dark curls fell across his troubled brow, but his eyes were as keen as a hawk, and his nerves steady. Despite the confident threat that he would lose, he had another outcome in mind. That was what he concentrated on, and let his anger fuel his determination.

Gilles London turned up dressed head to toe in black with a white shirt. His too was open at the neck, with the long sleeves buttoned at the cuffs. He wore it with a black waistcoat. He'd acquired a sword in a style that he was familiar with, and that was the agreed equal length to his challenger. He tested it by cutting it repeatedly through the still air.

Crispin Midwinter knew he was not only testing the sword, but testing his rival's nerve and trying to unsettle him. He failed on both accounts.

The air was calm, the silence heavy. As the dawn rose, filtering rays of light through the mist, the sun burned away the haze and clouds, leaving everything in sharp focus.

No apology was proposed to his challenger by Gilles London upon his arrival. An apology would've been accepted by Crispin Midwinter and settled the offence without combat.

Everything was set up properly, and each combatant had a second in attendance. No more, no less. Charmaine stayed safe within Blackhall, gazing out the window, watching from a distance. She saw the two figures, swords at the ready, face each other — and then the fierce clash of swords began.

Crispin Midwinter was the first to draw blood as he sliced through his opponent's sleeve. The razor sharp blade cut across the top of Mr. London's sword arm, through the linen fabric of his shirt to the bare flesh. It was a swift slash that did not slice to the bone, but was enough to cause a gash of red on the shirt sleeve, and wipe the smirk off Gilles London's arrogant face.

The clash of metal sounded in the air, louder now as the fight notched up to a dangerous level where Mr. London was well prepared to cut Mr. Midwinter down without mercy.

Seeing the hatred in his rival's eyes, Mr. Midwinter defended and attacked with every move strong and swift.

They each silently knew they were equally matched in terms of skill, though Mr. Midwinter had regular and recent practise on his side, while Mr. London was considered to be one of the best for a gentleman of his type.

It would come down to two things — fire and skill. Whoever could balance the two, the fight and ferocity in equal measures, would win the day.

Mr. Midwinter suffered a painful cut across his forearm, but fought on with greater determination, as the wound dripped blood and the flesh was ripped open.

Tears trickled down from Charmaine Midwinter's soulful eyes as she willed Crispin to beat Gilles. But deep down she blamed herself for having been fooled for even a second by the charlatan's false smiles. If her ego had not been so flattered by his attentions, her cousin's life would not be in jeopardy. It was her fault. She blamed no one but herself.

Mr. Midwinter gained the upper hand repeatedly, injuring Mr. London again as his blade cut across his chest and shoulder.

Mr. Midwinter stepped back, giving the seconds a moment to agree to consider the combat.

Knowing he would surely be cut down further, Mr. London nodded, accepting his defeat.

Mr. Midwinter nodded firmly. Honour had been attained to his satisfaction. The duel ended bloody, but satisfied.

Mr. London, accompanied by his second, left the scene, and was resigned to leave and go home to Bath.

Mr. Midwinter thanked his second, and then walked back to Blackhall, where he was met by a tearful and yet smiling Miss Midwinter. She threw her arms around him, careful not to hurt his wound. They went inside the house where he was attended to by staff.

Cleaned up and bandaged, the day had barely started, when Mr. Midwinter sat down to eat breakfast with Charmaine.

Her tears had dried, and now all that remained was her relieved and grateful smile as they ate breakfast together with the sun shining in the tall windows of Blackhall.

'We should let more light into this house,' Mr. Midwinter said, gazing around him.

Blackhall was well named, dark in architecture and in the dark drapes that shuttered out a lot of the light. His grandfather had preferred a sombre decor, and in his later years, the shuttering had become more intense as he lived a darker existence.

Miss Midwinter nodded. 'This house would benefit from more sunlight and a brighter decor. It has the potential to be truly beautiful.'

Agreeing to make plans for this, they smiled at each other and finished their breakfast with light chatter. The Gilles London affair would be part of the past. As far as Crispin Midwinter was concerned, the scoundrel didn't merit another moment of their time.

Rupert Feingold rode immediately to Blackhall on hearing of the duel, hoping neither challenger was badly injured.

Upon his arrival, he was led into the dining room by a member of staff, and announced.

Crispin Midwinter stood up to welcome him. 'I trust you heard of the challenge?'

'I've just received the news. And the outcome?'

'Gilles London was slightly injured, nothing he will not remedy,' Mr. Midwinter explained. 'He is to leave here and go home to Bath this day.'

Rupert Feingold sighed with relief. 'Thank goodness. I felt responsible for initiating the duel, putting you in such a situation.'

Mr. Feingold shook his head. 'No, you did the right thing telling me of the man's character.' He glanced at Miss Midwinter. 'Had you not, I fear he would've further compromised my cousin. Her trust in him was unrewarded by his devious intentions.'

'His reputation for being a womaniser is known in certain circles,' said Mr. Feingold. 'We thankfully were informed before he did any great damage to the ladies in our neighbourhood.'

Charmaine Midwinter looked quite pale, for although the events had ended well, the whole situation, especially her concern that her cousin could've been cut down by such a charlatan, had taken its toll on her.

'You look pale, Charmaine,' said Mr. Midwinter. 'Are you unwell?'

She stood up, feeling slightly light headed. She'd been distraught watching the duel, and barely ate anything for breakfast, sipping only a cup of tea. The previous night her anxiousness caused her to refuse supper. Overall, it had weakened her to the point that she suddenly felt faint.

Mr. Feingold rushed to her side and caught her before she fell to the floor. As pale and fragile as she'd ever been, she gave in and allowed him to sweep her up in his capable arms and carry her to her room.

Mr. Midwinter led the way, calling to staff to send for a physician immediately, but as Mr. Feingold laid her gently on her bed, she revived enough to tell them that all she needed was some tea, a light meal and rest — and most of all, to relax now that the duel was finished to their satisfaction.

'Are you sure?' Mr. Feingold asked her, leaning down to study her pale face. 'I will fetch someone immediately to tend to you.'

'No, thank you, sir,' she said. 'I'm simply overcome from the concern that Crispin could've been badly hurt, or worse, because of my foolish behaviour with Mr. London.'

'You are not to blame,' Mr. Midwinter told her. 'Gilles London is the only culprit in this whole unfortunate affair.'

'But everything is settled now, so you should too,' Mr. Feingold assured her.

'I'm grateful for your kindness, sir.' She smiled at Mr. Feingold, and for a moment she saw a greater handsomeness in him than when she'd first met him at the ball. He was a fine looking gentleman with an amiable nature and ready smile. She valued those qualities far more than any frivolous flattery.

Tea and biscuits were served to her in her room, and one of the staff, a capable woman, tended to her while Mr. Midwinter and Mr. Feingold sat in the drawing room discussing the matter.

'I think she's slightly shocked by the whole unfortunate business,' said Mr. Midwinter.

Rupert Feingold agreed. 'Once the realisation that you are safe settles her nerves, I'm sure she will be fine. But if I may, I'd like to call on her, on both of you, to enquire if the situation has been remedied.'

'That's very thoughtful of you, and I look forward to seeing you again.'

Rupert Feingold left Blackhall and rode back to Heather Park. Dark clouds swept across the sky, blocking out the summer sunshine. The vast estate of Heather Park with its imposing house was cast in shadows, and he arrived moments before the rain poured down.

He hurried inside, shaking off a few drops of rain from the shoulders of his tailcoat.

Raine Feingold ran to meet him. At first he feared that something was wrong, but it was only her concern for his safety at Blackhall.

'Is the duel over?' she asked anxiously.

'It is. Neither man was badly hurt, though Mr. London was injured enough to warrant acknowledging his defeat.'

'Thank goodness. I've been so concerned. I wondered what would happen if Mr. London had beaten Crispin Midwinter, and you had walked into Blackhall. I was worried Mr. London would then fight with you.'

'You're distressing yourself over something that did not happen, or will ever happen. Mr. London is leaving for Bath. We will not see him again. The matter is dealt with.'

He went on to tell her about Miss Midwinter.

'How dreadful, though I understand her distress. I would be happy to accompany you to Blackhall to visit her.'

He nodded. 'That's an ideal suggestion.'

As the rain hit off the windows of Heather Park, they gazed out at the stormy day.

Raine Feingold shivered. 'I will feel better when Mr. Hunter comes home. Nothing feels settled with him away in Bath.'

'He's gone to London now. I received a letter early this morning. I hadn't a chance to tell you before I rode to Blackhall.'

'London? He's gone home to London?'

'Yes, but only for a short visit.'

She watched the rain pour down the windows. 'Do you believe he'll be able to settle here?'

'Yes, why shouldn't he?'

'He loved London. We all did.'

'I'm very happy to be here in the country at Heather Park. Very happy indeed.'

'So am I, and I'm looking forward to Evelyn Ashby coming home so that I can enjoy her company for painting.'

'Miss Ashby will be back soon too,' he assured her. 'And we have the ball at Seaforth to look forward to.'

She smiled, remembering the ball was underway. In all the fuss, she'd forgotten about it. 'That's right. A ball will surely brighten everyone again.' She glanced out the window at the pouring rain. 'Even if the weather is inclement.'

'It's just a summer storm, and will disappear as swiftly as it arrived,' he told her.

Trusting his words, she smiled and continued to gaze out the window at the storm.

Evelyn looked out the window of the carriage as it drove through Bath. The busy streets were filled with people carrying umbrellas or dashing from shops into carriages. The rain shaded everything in tones of grey.

Her father sat opposite her reading the newspaper. His business in Bath was done. The trip had been successful, and he would not need to come here again for a while. He'd written a few letters to her mother, and she imagined she'd hear all about the contents once she arrived home.

'I sent a letter to your mother last night. It'll arrive after we do,' he said. 'But she does love receiving letters, so I hope she will be happy with the letters I've written.'

'I'm certain she will be delighted,' Evelyn assured him.

He smiled and then began reading his newspaper again, while Evelyn took a last look at Bath as they headed away. And she wondered about Mr. Hunter. He'd be home in London. She was looking forward to telling her mother and her sisters all the news and gossip — and relaxing. She imagined very little had happened since she'd been away. She was definitely looking forward to a quieter time at home.

Parcels of fabric, trims, hats, accessories and all manner of pretty things, including the artificial flowers, were strapped on to the roof of the carriage. She couldn't wait to give the gifts to her mother and sisters.

Evelyn's aunt had insisted that she accept a couple of new dresses, including the lovely lilac one. It would be perfect for the next ball, she mused, the one at Seaforth. And she thought about Captain Domenic DeGrey, her first encounter with him as she walked to the coast. Her heart gave an involuntary flutter as she remembered his sculptured features, the rich dark hair and the skill with which he'd ridden off at speed through the trees.

She hadn't managed to dance with him at the Heather Park ball, but she was sure she would during the ball at Seaforth. She sighed, wondering where her heart would lead her. Those intense green eyes of Captain DeGrey had sent her heart fluttering when he'd gazed at her. He looked so handsome at the recent ball, and if she hadn't left early she would've liked to have danced with him.

The carriage juddered, shaking her out of her wayward thoughts. But then she started thinking about Captain DeGrey again, wondering if he really was planning to settle down at Seaforth. Or would a settled life elude him? He'd been away for four years, sailing the seas, having adventures. Would he feel the same as Mr. Hunter? Would he miss his past life? She wasn't sure. They were two different gentlemen, each with their own adventurous pasts, one in London and one at sea.

'What did you make of your time in Bath then, Evelyn?' her father asked her, folding his paper and tucking it aside.

‘I was happy to see aunt and uncle again,’ she replied. ‘My aunt has been so kind, insisting I take the new dresses home with me. I had such fun in her company.’

Her father smiled and nodded up, indicating the parcels that were strapped to the carriage roof. ‘And you’ve been busy shopping.’

Evelyn smiled at him. ‘Indeed I have. Thank you for taking me with you.’

‘I almost insisted you stay at the Heather Park ball and I would travel on my own to Bath. It was such a fine ball.’

‘I’m happy I decided to go with you,’ she assured him.

He smiled over at her. ‘Perhaps you’ll travel with me again to Bath, or London.’

At the mention of London her thoughts jarred her. She thought of Sabastien Hunter. An ache of longing for something she wasn’t even sure she wanted, swept through her heart.

‘Yes, perhaps I shall,’ she said, gazing out at the last view of Bath that looked like a watercolour in the rain.

CHAPTER EIGHT

The sea was wild along the coast at Seaforth. The rainstorm added to the atmosphere. The shades of grey in the rainy sky tinted the sea dark silver, with the froth only marginally paler.

Captain Domenic DeGrey stood on the upstairs balcony of his bedroom, looking out at the day, sensing a change in the circumstances at Seaforth as the ball was to be held there soon. He was waiting — waiting for Evelyn Ashby to come home from Bath. And when she did, would she make an announcement of her impending engagement to Sabastien Hunter?

Since he'd heard the local gossip that Mr. Hunter had gone to Bath shortly after the ball at Heather Park, he'd barely settled, wondering if his sudden trip to Bath was purely business or if his intention was to pursue Miss Ashby. His heart twisted at the thought that Mr. Hunter would secure her affections. He feared he'd have to fight to make his own intentions known to her. Not in a duel like the one everyone was talking about between Crispin Midwinter and Gilles London. No, this would be a fight to win through all the barriers being thrown in his path in his bid to tell her he loved her. He loved her dearly, and had for years.

The sea air blew through his dark hair and the shirt he wore, unbuttoned at the neck and worn with a fitted waistcoat. He'd been dressing for the day ahead when news had arrived on the duel at Blackhall and the distress caused to Miss Charmaine Midwinter. If he'd known the underhanded character of Mr. London, he'd have dealt with him swiftly himself. Thankfully, Mr. Midwinter had taken charge of the issue and it had been resolved satisfactorily. Nonetheless, damage had been done. Mr. Midwinter had been slightly injured, a wound he would no doubt brush off without concern. But apparently it was fortunate that Rupert Feingold had been on hand to catch Miss Midwinter as she fainted and carried her to her room. The trouble that Mr. London had initiated would not be forgotten lightly.

Stepping in from the balcony, he knotted his cravat around his neck, put on his long boots, and prepared to ride to Blackhall to offer his assistance. Crispin Midwinter was in a similar position to him in that they were both without longstanding friends, family or reliable acquaintances in the neighbourhood. Whether they would become good friends or not, he felt it was his duty to call upon Mr. Midwinter at Blackhall that day.

Wearing a long, dark coat that shielded him against the worst of the rain, and a dark hat, he rode his chestnut horse to Blackhall. He passed no one on the country road, as it seemed that everyone was sheltering sensibly indoors against the downpour. The rain did not deter him. Days and nights sailing in stormy seas had taught him to handle all manner of harsh weather. A rainy day here was mild in comparison to the huge waves the ships he'd sailed on had cut through without altering their course. His intention was to visit Blackhall. Rain would not dampen his resolve.

A carriage drove up to Blackhall as Captain DeGrey rode to the house. Five ladies alighted from the carriage, shielded with umbrellas by two members of staff.

Lady Thornbee and her daughter, Octavia, were the first to step from the carriage. Then Mrs. Ashby and her daughters Annabel and Primrose hurried inside the house to shelter from the rain. All of them wore coats or capes and hats.

From under one of the black umbrellas, he noticed Primrose glance back at him. She nodded and then scurried inside with the others.

One of the staff then tended to Captain DeGrey's horse while he followed the ladies. His long coat dripped as he stood in the large hallway of the mansion, waiting to be announced to Mr. Midwinter.

They all appeared to be there due to the altercation between Mr. Midwinter and Mr. London.

'What a dreadful business this is,' Mrs. Ashby commented to Captain DeGrey.

'Indeed it is,' he replied. 'Most unfortunate.'

'We came right away when we heard how distressed Miss Midwinter was,' Mrs. Ashby told him. 'Lady Thornbee was kind enough to offer us a ride in her carriage. Mr. Ashby and Evelyn are still in Bath, though they are due home soon.'

Captain DeGrey's heart jolted at the mention of Evelyn, and he held his breath, wondering if Mrs. Ashby would make any mention of Mr. Hunter. But she did not. She didn't even hint of any attachment. This bolstered his spirits immensely.

He smiled at Mrs. Ashby. 'I trust their trip to Bath has been pleasant.'

'It has. Mr. Ashby has written to me every day, and his business there has been successful.'

'And your daughter, is she well?' he asked Mrs. Ashby.

'Oh yes. Evelyn's aunt has been spoiling her and they've gone shopping every day.'

'Evelyn will have bought fabric and items for sewing,' said Primrose, knowing her sister well. She gazed up into the captain's handsome face as he listened to her, his green eyes looking intense.

'Miss Midwinter has been sewing with us every day this week,' Mrs. Ashby said to him. 'That's why we're so upset for her and the trouble Mr. London has caused her.' She shook her head. 'The poor dear.'

And all the while Octavia Thornbee eyed Captain DeGrey, thinking that he looked even more handsome, soaked but strong, than when she'd seen him at the ball.

He'd acknowledged all five ladies, but paid no particular attention to the unsmiling Octavia Thornbee. As before, he noticed how lovely Miss Primrose was, and Miss Annabel.

Before they could continue their conversation, a member of staff led them into the drawing room where they were announced and welcomed by Crispin Midwinter and Charmaine Midwinter.

Miss Midwinter was seated by the fireside. The fire was lit and gave warmth to that area of the room. The rainstorm had washed the heat right out of the summer's day, leaving a damp chill that the fire helped to alleviate.

'She looks rather pale,' Lady Thornbee observed, whispering to Mrs. Ashby.

Mrs. Ashby nodded and walked over to talk to Miss Midwinter.

'How are you, my dear?' Mrs. Ashby asked her, leaning down and speaking with gentle concern.

'I am fine now,' Miss Midwinter replied.

Lady Thornbee spoke up, addressing Mr. Midwinter. 'Your cousin looks too pale to be fine. Has she been properly attended to? I could recommend my personal physician to take a look at her.'

'Thank you for your kind concern, Lady Thornbee,' Miss Midwinter replied on his behalf. 'I think this rain has dampened my spirits too when I most needed a day of summer sunshine.'

'The sunshine will be bright again soon,' Mrs. Ashby assured Miss Midwinter. 'These rainstorms never last. They sweep in, cause a dampness of spirit, and then disappear, leaving the sunlight to brighten us up again.'

Miss Midwinter nodded and smiled, grateful for the reassurance.

'In the meantime, you are welcome to join us at Heathfield,' said Mrs. Ashby. 'We are embroidering new patterns with lots of pretty flowers. If you're feeling well enough to travel by carriage, we'd be delighted to have you spend the day with us.'

This offer appealed greatly to Miss Midwinter and she glanced at her cousin for his approval. She didn't want to seem as if his company had not brightened her mood. On the contrary, Crispin had been attentive and kind, even though his wound was still healing.

'I think that's a splendid idea,' Mr. Midwinter said, thinking that the company of the Ashby ladies and sewing, which Charmaine loved, was just the tonic she needed. 'I'll have one of our carriages take you there.'

The smiles from the ladies, apart from Octavia, showed that they were happy with this suggestion.

'May I enquire about your injury,' Captain DeGrey said to Mr. Midwinter.

Mr. Midwinter nodded in thanks. 'I am certain the wound will heal fine, but I thank you for asking.'

Neither of them wished to dwell on the details of the duel in front of the ladies, especially Miss Midwinter whose cheeks were now showing a slight flush of colour. In part it was due to wanting to join in the sewing and spend time with her new friends. But it was also the masculine presence of Captain DeGrey that sent her pulse racing.

Miss Midwinter sighed and bit her lip, unsure about leaving her cousin on his own. 'What about you, Crispin? Will you be fine here on your own?' Blackhall had sufficient staff, but she referred to social company.

A thought struck Mr. Midwinter and he smiled at his idea. 'Perhaps I could persuade Captain DeGrey to join me for a game or two of cards before he leaves.'

'Yes, I would be happy to join you,' Captain DeGrey confirmed. It would've been churlish to refuse, and he didn't want to. He enjoyed playing cards and a few games with a likeminded gentleman would be welcome.

Miss Midwinter smiled, cheered that her cousin now had company.

Octavia spoke up. 'I would prefer to join the gentlemen. I like to sew, but I love to play cards and other games.'

Mrs. Ashby didn't doubt it. This had been quite a bold move on Octavia's part. But now she was to be left in the company of the gentlemen while Primrose and Annabel went home. A very clever move, Mrs. Ashby secretly acknowledged.

As it wasn't suitable for a young lady to be left without a chaperone under the present circumstances, Lady Thornbee decided to stay too.

Mrs. Ashby smiled at Mr. Midwinter. 'Later, you're welcome to join us for dinner. You too Captain.'

'Yes, I'd be delighted,' Mr. Midwinter was quick to reply, glancing at Annabel. He'd glanced at her several times, admiring her beauty and wishing to become better acquainted with her. Dinner at Heathfield would afford him this opportunity, so he was keen to accept.

The invitation was less tempting to Captain DeGrey as he had a lot of work to attend to, most of it revolving around the arranging of the ball at Seaforth.

'Evelyn should hopefully be home by then,' Mrs. Ashby added. 'Or later on, for supper.'

'I'd love to join you for dinner,' Captain DeGrey said without further hesitation. The thought of having dinner with Evelyn Ashby filled him with excitement. Not that anyone in their company detected a hint of his inner joy.

Mrs. Ashby didn't extend the dinner invitation to Lady Thornbee and Octavia because she knew that Lady Thornbee and her daughter had a dinner engagement planned.

Primrose and Annabel bowed and smiled at the gentlemen before leaving.

The carriage awaited them outside the front entrance of Blackhall.

Mrs. Ashby whispered to her daughters as they walked outside. 'That was a shrewd move by Octavia. She's a clever one.'

Annabel and Primrose nodded.

Miss Midwinter overheard, but did not take offence or judge them on their observation. 'I agree,' she told them.

Mrs. Ashby gasped at having been caught making such a remark, but Miss Midwinter's knowing smile wiped away her concerns.

Shielded by staff holding umbrellas, Mrs. Ashby, her daughters and Miss Midwinter, stepped into the Blackhall carriage and were driven off.

The rain still fell, blurring the view of Blackhall, as Primrose looked out the carriage window. Secretly, she wished to have stayed there with Octavia to be in the company of Captain DeGrey. There was something about him that attracted her deepest senses, and yet, she didn't sense he felt the same about her. Time would tell if her attraction to him would be reciprocated.

Mr. Midwinter gazed out the window of the drawing room at the carriage heading away. He thought about Miss Annabel. She'd looked beautiful. Even in the rainy day, she'd brightened Blackhall more than a summer afternoon. Her bright blue eyes, soft skin and beautiful features, melted his heart. He loved the way her blonde locks framed her face below the brim of her pretty bonnet. Miss Annabel had captured his attention more than any other woman he'd ever met.

As the carriage disappeared into the rain, Mr. Midwinter smiled at his guests. 'Right, shall we play a game of cards?' He ushered them over to a table in a corner of the drawing room.

Octavia sat facing both gentlemen, making sure her cold beauty could be admired by them while they played. She found card games boring, and far preferred sewing, but cards was not the game she had in mind.

Lady Thornbee had equal disinterest in card games, but approved of Octavia's moves to secure the acquaintance and company of Mr. Midwinter and Captain DeGrey. She'd noticed the way Mr. Midwinter looked at Miss Annabel. There was a definite attraction between them, but Octavia's games had some enticing moves that she was sure he'd find hard to resist. Captain DeGrey was difficult to fathom. Had he noticed the way Miss Primrose admired him? If he had not, where were his musings? What woman occupied his thoughts?

'Shall we begin?' Mr. Midwinter said, dealing out the cards.

Octavia almost smiled. The game had already begun.

Sewing, embroidery, floral patterns and fabric were scattered around the parlour as Mrs. Ashby, Annabel, Primrose and Charmaine Midwinter stitched and chatted. Their sewing boxes were spilling over with embroidery patterns, thread and ribbons. Gossip was shared, and the laughter had cheered Miss Midwinter. Her upset was completely forgotten. All was well and happy in the cosy Heathfield household.

'Are you staying permanently at Blackhall?' Annabel asked Miss Midwinter.

'My plans are not settled. Our families live in Oxfordshire, and I've been friends with Crispin since we were children. So when the inheritance fell to him, our families suggested someone should accompany him to Blackhall. As the gentlemen were all attached with families of their own to attend to, or busy with business, the task was put on to me.' She sighed. 'We women never have anything to occupy our times as gentlemen do. As I was unattached, I travelled with Crispin, to help him settle into his new life here, and offer a woman's perspective on how to lift Blackhall from its rather gloomy ambiance.'

'I do hope you'll say awhile,' said Mrs. Ashby. 'It's always fortunate to make new friends.'

'I am staying for the summer,' Miss Midwinter told them. 'Depending on circumstances, I may extend my stay.'

The Ashby ladies smiled, pleased to know that they had her company for the summer season.

Primrose had given her a lovely bluebell pattern to embroider, and helped her select the thread.

'You're quite an accomplished embroiderer, Miss Midwinter,' Primrose said, watching her stitch the floral pattern on to a white linen handkerchief.

'I love to embroider,' Miss Midwinter said, satin stitching the bluebell petals. 'But I've never had such a range of patterns, thread and fabric to work with. I love these flower patterns that your sister,

Evelyn has drawn. Her art is exquisite. I am not at all accomplished at art.'

'Neither am I,' Primrose confessed. 'But I do love to embroider flowers.'

'I wish I could draw and design like Evelyn,' Annabel said, sighing.

'Do you play any instruments?' Mrs. Ashby asked Miss Midwinter. 'I noticed there was a beautiful piano forte in the drawing room at Blackhall.'

'I don't play, but I do love to dance,' said Miss Midwinter. 'Crispin has promised to plan the ball at Blackhall after the one at Seaforth.' She paused, then asked, 'Have you known Captain DeGrey long?'

Mrs. Ashby shook her head. 'No, we only met him at the Heather Park ball, but Mr. Ashby knew his grandfather, Admiral DeGrey.'

Miss Midwinter was eager to find out more about Captain DeGrey. 'He seems to be in a similar circumstance to my cousin, Crispin. Both are young men and have inherited substantial estates and properties.'

'So has Sabastien Hunter,' Mrs. Ashby added. 'All fine young gentlemen with inheritances. Though I suppose Captain DeGrey hasn't inherited Seaforth. He's in charge of it while his grandfather is sailing abroad.'

'I would think that the captain will inherit Seaforth,' said Miss Midwinter.

'Oh, yes,' Mrs. Ashby replied. 'He told me he's keen to settle there. I presume he'll be looking to find himself a wife.'

'Did he mention his desire to get married?' Miss Midwinter asked, trying not to show her particular interest in him.

Mrs. Ashby nodded. 'He did. He told me this at the ball. I feel he's more of a settled character than Mr. Sabastien Hunter.' She shrugged. 'But I do not know them well enough yet, so the balls at Seaforth and Blackhall will give us ample chance to find out more about their plans.'

'He is very handsome and quite dashing,' Primrose gushed, letting slip her admiration for the captain.

The others giggled, causing Primrose to blush. 'Mr. Hunter is handsome too, as is his friend, Rupert Feingold,' she said, trying to sound as if she was not particularly interested in Captain DeGrey.

'Mr. Feingold is very pleasing,' Miss Midwinter said, thinking how strong and attractive he'd been when he'd helped her at Blackhall.

'Did he really catch you before you fell in a faint, lift you up and carry you to your room?' Primrose asked her.

'He did,' Miss Midwinter confirmed. 'He was very strong and capable. And kind. I like a man that is kind and has a steady, cheerful character.'

'Mr. Ashby has all those qualities,' said Mrs. Ashby. 'I hope that my daughters are as fortunate to find a partner like I did.'

'I'm only ever going to marry for love,' said Annabel.

'So will I,' Primrose added.

'I would not marry for any other reason,' Miss Midwinter added.

'Well, there are quite a few suitable gentlemen here now,' said Mrs. Ashby. 'I expect there to be a flurry of engagements before the end of the season.'

'So soon?' Miss Midwinter said, frowning.

'Oh, yes,' Mrs. Ashby nodded. 'I wouldn't be surprised if some of you will make attachments to the gentlemen.' She smiled and continued her sewing, embroidering lilac flowers and heliotrope. She gave them a teasing smile.

The young women giggled and smiled.

'You tease us so, Mrs. Ashby,' Miss Midwinter said, shaking her head and smiling.

Mrs. Ashby continued stitching her embroidery. 'Perhaps a little, but with such beautiful young women and handsome men available, I'm sure attachments will be made.'

'Shall we play a game, for fun?' Primrose said, setting aside her embroidery.

'What type of game?' asked Miss Midwinter.

Primrose started folding pieces of paper and writing several men's names on them. She spoke the names aloud as she wrote each one on a piece of the paper. The names were: Sabastien Hunter, Rupert Feingold, Crispin Midwinter, and Captain Domenic DeGrey. She included pieces that said, Mr. No One, Mr. Not This Year, and Mr. Yet to Meet.

The Ashby ladies had played this game before, but Miss Midwinter had not played it. 'How do we play this game?'

Primrose folded all the pieces of paper and put them in one of the bonnets they were making. 'Close your eyes, put your hand in and pick out a piece of paper. Read the name, or message on it, but don't say anything. Remember the name, fold the paper up again and drop it back into the bonnet. We each have the same chance to pick from all the gentlemen.'

Miss Midwinter laughed. 'Has this game ever come to fruition? Has anyone married a name they'd chosen at random?'

'Yes,' said Primrose. 'But it's only a light game for fun.'

With all of them set to select a piece of paper, the game began.

Miss Midwinter was the first to select a name. She reached into the bonnet, rummaged around, smiling, enjoying the fun, and then picked out a name. She read the name, hid her surprise, and then added it into the bonnet again.

Miss Annabel was the second to play, followed by Primrose.

Primrose read the name, looked delighted, folded the paper and put it back.

'Now we reveal the name, one by one, starting with you, Miss Midwinter,' Primrose prompted her.

Taking a deep breath and trying not to blush, Miss Midwinter said, 'Captain Domenic DeGrey.'

Gasps and giggled followed, then it was Annabel's turn. She announced, 'Crispin Midwinter.'

Miss Midwinter clapped. 'Oh, I must tell Crispin. He will be so amused.'

'No,' Annabel scolded Miss Midwinter playfully. 'You cannot reveal our secrets to the gentlemen. It would be too embarrassing. And they'd think we were silly playing such games.'

Nodding, Miss Midwinter smiled.

Now it was Primrose's turn to tell. 'Captain Domenic DeGrey.'

'We're going to be rivals for his affections,' Miss Midwinter joked with Primrose.

Mrs. Ashby smiled. 'What about poor Mr. Hunter and Mr. Feingold? No romance for them?'

'I've yet to select one for Evelyn,' said Primrose. 'She gave the papers a thorough mix in the bonnet, and then picked one out and read it. 'Captain Domenic DeGrey.'

'What?' Mrs. Ashby said, laughing. 'Captain DeGrey is going to be a very popular and busy man — and Mr. Midwinter.'

‘Excuse me, ma’am,’ Tilsy announced, ‘Mr. Crispin Midwinter and Captain Domenic DeGrey have arrived.’

The two gentlemen stood in the doorway of the drawing room having heard the last few moments of the conversation as Tilsy attempted to gain Mrs. Ashby’s attention. But the women had been so steeped in chatter and laughter that Mrs. Ashby hadn’t realised they were there.

The women were startled, embarrassed, smiling, blushing, all in equal measures, realising they’d been caught by two of the gentlemen they’d included in their game.

Mr. Midwinter addressed his cousin. ‘Whatever mischief are you up to, Charmaine?’ He smiled, awaiting her explanation.

CHAPTER NINE

'Nothing,' Charmaine Midwinter told her cousin, trying not to smile.

'Hmmm, how fortunate you are to be amused by nothing,' Crispin Midwinter remarked.

Miss Midwinter sighed and relented. 'It's women's secrets.'

'Ah, that I can accept,' said Mr. Midwinter. He glanced at Captain DeGrey. 'Do you agree?'

'I do, though I suspect I'm agreeing to something that will get me into as much mischief as the ladies have been enjoying,' he said.

'We're man enough to chance it though, aren't we?' Mr. Midwinter encouraged him lightly.

'We are, though I wonder why I'm suspicious of their motives.' Captain DeGrey gave a knowing smile.

Mrs. Ashby changed the subject. She put her sewing down and stood up. 'We weren't expecting your company until later,' she said, sounding cheerful.

'I hope we are not intruding on you,' Mr. Midwinter said to her.

'No, we're delighted to have you join us,' Mrs. Ashby said, gesturing for the gentlemen to come in. 'Please be seated, if you can find somewhere that is not occupied with our sewing,' she added jokingly, sitting back down.

Mr. Midwinter sat down beside Miss Midwinter while Captain DeGrey took a seat near Mrs. Ashby.

'Did you enjoy your card games?' Mrs. Ashby asked them.

The men exchanged a tense glance, then Mr. Midwinter replied. 'We did. Lady Thornbee and Miss Octavia are adept at playing games.' There was an underlying meaning to his words that wasn't missed by the ladies.

Mrs. Ashby nodded. 'I'm pleased you found their company...enlightening.'

Another glance shot between the gentlemen.

Reluctant to discuss the game playing, Captain DeGrey showed a sudden interest in Mrs. Ashby's embroidery that she was working on. 'Beautiful embroidery,' he remarked.

'Oh, thank you,' she said. 'These are Evelyn's designs. She designed these flowers.'

While Captain DeGrey admired the designs, Mr. Midwinter whispered quickly to his cousin. 'We had to make our excuses to leave Miss Thornbee's company.'

Miss Midwinter's eyes widened. 'What happened?' she whispered insistently.

There wasn't a moment to explain, as it was evident to those present that they were confiding about Octavia Thornbee.

The gentlemen enjoyed the company of the ladies, and the atmosphere in the Ashby household was cheerful as they had tea and chatted about Captain DeGrey's plans for the forthcoming ball at Seaforth.

'I've never organised a ball,' Captain DeGrey admitted, 'but the staff are helping to handle the necessary arrangements.'

'Have you set a date yet?' Annabel asked him.

'I should be able to confirm the date very soon,' he promised. If Evelyn Ashby arrived home from Bath in time for dinner, he'd announce it that evening. He wanted to be sure that she would be there.

Mrs. Ashby looked out the window. The rain had drizzled to a halt earlier in the day. 'I hope the rain hasn't held up Mr. Ashby's carriage. I expected him to be home this evening, but if the weather has delayed their progress, they may have to stay overnight in another town and travel again in the morning.'

Captain DeGrey felt disappointed. His hopes were high that he'd dine with Miss Ashby that evening. But her safety was utmost in his concerns.

The discussion circled back to the ball at Seaforth, with Primrose enquiring if Captain DeGrey had a preference for the dances and music.

'My tastes in music are wide ranging,' he told her. 'I'm keen to include many of the popular dances and music to ensure the ball is lively and fun.'

This remark was met with great delight by everyone present.

'The musicians that played at Heather Park have been secured to play at Seaforth,' he added.

Mrs. Ashby nodded approvingly. 'They were very good.'

'As Charmaine has made me promise to hold a ball at Blackhall,' Mr. Midwinter began, 'I will have to start planning too.'

'I will help you,' Miss Midwinter assured him.

'I'm sure both events will be equally wonderful,' said Mrs. Ashby. 'But what matters most for a successful ball is the company.'

'I wholeheartedly agree,' Mr. Midwinter said firmly. 'Without the best of company, true success cannot be had.'

'The company of good friends and loved ones is what definitely matters,' Captain DeGrey added.

Primrose found herself liking Captain DeGrey more and more. His attitude was admiral.

Miss Midwinter was quite mesmerised by Captain DeGrey's company. She believed the things he said to be true. There was no sense of falseness in his words. Her only hesitation was his disinterest in her, in the sense of attraction. He appeared to be happy in her company, but there was a distance in his expression. Those green eyes of his often had a faraway look to them. Whatever was he thinking about, she wondered.

Mrs. Ashby had noticed this too. Mr. Midwinter seemed to be very interested in Annabel. But the captain, although pleasant, paid no special attention to Primrose, Annabel or Charmaine. This was a bit disappointing, for she sincerely loved to see young romance flourishing. But she contented herself with the budding connection being made between Mr. Midwinter and Annabel. They'd make a fine couple, she mused, and she would help nurture such an attachment.

As the day faded into evening, dinner was served. They sat around the table and were about to start their meal when a carriage pulled up outside.

'Oh, there's Mr. Ashby!' Mrs. Ashby cried, jumping up and scurrying to greet him.

Primrose and Annabel hurried too.

Captain DeGrey's heart soared as he saw Evelyn Ashby walk into the room as her mother and sisters fussed over her.

'It rained for half the journey,' Miss Ashby told them, shrugging off her cloak and taking off her hat. 'I feared we'd be held up, but thankfully we're home.'

The bustling and activity of the welcome home made Captain DeGrey view the scene as if apart from it. But this was the type of happy life he hoped for. For all the wealth he had, there really wasn't anything so necessary as the company of loved ones.

Amid the chatter and smiles, Miss Ashby was delighted to see they had company. 'Captain DeGrey,' she said, nodding to him.

'Miss Ashby,' he replied. His polite and calm exterior hid his longing to wrap her in his arms and welcome her home.

She then glanced at their other guests in anticipation of being introduced.

'Evelyn, this is Crispin Midwinter from Blackhall, and his cousin, Charmaine Midwinter,' said Mrs. Ashby. 'They were at the Heather Park ball, but you didn't have a chance to make their acquaintance.'

The three of them acknowledged each other politely.

'And this is my husband, Mr. Ashby,' she said to the Midwinters.

While his wife fussed around him, he smiled at their guests.

Staff unloaded the carriage and carried their luggage inside.

Tilsy brought more food to the table and set it down.

'We were just about to have dinner,' Mrs. Ashby said to her husband and Evelyn.

Everyone was seated, with Mr. Ashby at the head of the table. Evelyn sat opposite Mr. Midwinter. Miss Annabel was seated to his right.

Captain DeGrey sat beside Evelyn. But then Miss Midwinter seated herself next to him, so he now had one of them on either side of him.

Miss Midwinter did her utmost to engage his full attention, but although he answered her politely, it was Miss Ashby he was interested in.

'Did you enjoy Bath?' Captain DeGrey said, sounding calm and steady, while his heart thundered in his chest. He could barely believe that he was sitting so close beside her. All these years he'd imagined how enthralled he'd be if he was in her company. Now, he could see the silky amber highlights in her strawberry blonde hair, admire her fair complexion, and see her smile. A smile that lit his heart with joy. Every time her beautiful green eyes looked at him, he felt such love and longing for her.

'It was very pleasant, and I was happy to see my aunt and uncle,' said Evelyn. 'But I am not suited to living in such a busy place, and found myself wanting to be home.'

'I'm pleased to hear it,' said Captain DeGrey.

She looked into his stunning green eyes, feeling her heart flutter as she admired his handsomeness. His dark hair was swept back from his face, but a few stray strands gave him a roguish appearance. She could see the strength in him, the breadth of his shoulders as he sat there, giving her his full attention.

She thought about Sabastien Hunter, and found herself comparing him to Captain DeGrey. And comparing her feelings. The fluttering of her heart made her blush, and she tried to hide her reaction by starting to eat her dinner. She was genuinely hungry, but her appetite for dinner was less than her interest in the captain.

She felt the warmth of the cosy home atmosphere wrap her in its comfort, but she couldn't help feeling attracted to Captain DeGrey. Perhaps she was overtired from the trip, but she sensed that he was so pleased to be in her company, and that in itself made her smile at him.

Every time she smiled at him, his heart melted. He wondered if anyone noticed, but he tried staunchly to veil his reactions.

Talk of gifts of fabric, embroidery thread, and lots of other items, filled the air with excited chatter, and helped disguise his feelings for Miss Ashby. No one seemed to notice, except Miss Midwinter.

She astutely surmised that his heart was taken by Evelyn Ashby, and now realised that Miss Ashby was no doubt the one he'd been thinking about with that faraway look in his eyes. But according to Mrs. Ashby, Annabel and Primrose, they'd only been introduced to Captain DeGrey at the ball. So why did she feel that his heart was deeply entrenched in his love for Miss Ashby? For she sensed he did love her. No man looked at a women like that without his heart belonging to her.

Miss Midwinter blinked from her thoughts when Primrose addressed Captain DeGrey.

'What type of flowers do you have in the gardens at Seaforth?' Primrose asked him. 'I always thought that flowers found it hard to flourish close to the coast as the soil isn't ideal. But my father says the gardens are lovely with an extensive array of plants. I do love flowers.'

'The gardens have a beautiful selection of plants,' said Captain DeGrey. 'You're welcome to wander around and pick whatever flowers you like.'

This was the wrong thing to say, because Primrose misinterpreted his offer.

'Thank you for the invitation,' Primrose said, smiling at him. 'I shall definitely enjoy visiting you and your gardens.'

He realised his error, but now couldn't think of a way to retract the perceived invitation for fear of being ill–mannered.

While he'd spoken to Primrose, Mr. Midwinter had engaged Miss Ashby in conversation. He was now not part of it. To further separate him from speaking with Miss Ashby, her father remarked on his liking for Seaforth.

'The sea air is quite bracing. I recall being in the company of your grandfather some years ago. We stood in the garden in front of the house, and the wind was whipping along the coast.' Mr. Ashby continued to extol the benefits of the sea breeze. 'I felt thoroughly invigorated. You are lucky to be in charge of such a house and coastal estate.'

'I am very grateful for my present circumstances,' Captain DeGrey acknowledged. 'Seaforth is a wonderful home.'

'Lady Thornbee said the only thing it lacked was a lady,' Mr. Midwinter said, forgetting that he shouldn't mention what had happened earlier at Blackhall when they'd played cards. But in the relaxed company, he spoke freely, without malice. 'Lady Thornbee suggested the captain find himself a wife, marry and settle down. She also mentioned that her daughter, Octavia, was unattached.'

Miss Midwinter glared at her cousin, warning him not to reveal this matter so blatantly. For it was obvious to all in their company that Lady Thornbee had suggested her daughter was a suitable wife for Captain DeGrey.

Mrs. Ashby stepped in to rectify the conversation. 'Lady Thornbee is a long acquaintance of ours, but I believe she is somewhat overzealous to secure an advantageous marriage for her daughter, Octavia.'

'I like Lady Thornbee,' Mr. Ashby remarked. 'But she's too forthright in her display of her daughter's beauty and perceived value.'

'Mothers meddle,' Mrs. Ashby said, as if this exempted them from interfering. 'But I do try not to. Meddling in matters of the heart is a dangerous responsibility.'

Mr. Ashby stepped in to curtail this topic of conversation. 'Let's not talk about things that can only lead to mischief.' He smiled at his wife and daughters. 'There is always a surplus of that in this household.'

There were smiles all round for this was true.

'I'm sure we weren't up to any mischief,' Mrs. Ashby told him.

Mr. Ashby wasn't convinced. 'I'm equally sure I'll hear all about it tomorrow when you tell me whatever it is you've been up to.'

Mrs. Ashby relented with a smile. Her husband knew her too well for her to pretend that nothing of note had happened. She glanced at the conspiratorial company. They all knew it was not the time to tell Mr. Ashby and Evelyn about the duel. The atmosphere during dinner was light, and news of the vicious duel would dampen the happy mood.

Mr. Midwinter's wound was bandaged and hidden beneath the sleeve of his tailcoat, and he gave no hint that it ached slightly as it started to mend. He would not complain or dwell on it. Looking around the table at the convivial company was the only salve he needed. Sitting having dinner with Miss Annabel and her family was his delight.

Mr. Ashby helped himself to a slice of roast and encouraged Evelyn to tell them about the gifts she'd brought home for them.

'My aunt was so generous as to pay for all the gifts,' said Evelyn. 'And she also insisted on giving me two of her new dresses.' She smiled at the captain. 'So I will be spoiled as to which dress to wear to Seaforth ball. The lilac I think.'

Miss Midwinter spoke up. 'Crispin is planning a ball at Blackhall too.'

'Then I shall wear the blue one or the white dress I wore to Heather Park and accessorise it with the ribbons from Bath — and embroider more flowers and butterflies on it.'

'I hope you will show me your methods for adding embroidery to your dresses, for I would love to improve my skills,' said Miss Midwinter.

'Charmaine has been sewing with us here at Heathfield while you've been in Bath,' Evelyn's mother told her.

'I would be happy to instruct you,' Evelyn said to Charmaine.

Miss Midwinter smiled and nodded her thanks to Evelyn.

'What else did you bring from Bath?' Primrose asked excitedly.

'Beautiful fabric, lovely ribbon and trims from a wonderful haberdashery — and artificial flowers, including forget–me–nots and lily of the valley flowers that you can use as accessories for your dresses and bags for the balls.

Primrose's pale grey eyes widened with delight. 'Artificial flowers? That's perfect! Thank you, Evelyn.'

'Our aunt paid for everything,' Evelyn reminded her. 'I didn't use a penny of the allowance papa gave me.'

Mr. Ashby smiled to himself, hearing the tone of Evelyn's remark. 'You may keep the money, Evelyn, and spend it as you wish. I'm certain your favourite fabric draper's shop is where you'll receive the best value.'

Evelyn nodded and smiled. 'I shall share it with Annabel and Primrose.'

'I will write to our aunt in Bath to thank her,' said Primrose.

'She would appreciate a letter from you, my dear,' Mr. Ashby told her.

'I'm happy that you are not inclined to miss Bath or plan to move there,' Captain DeGrey said to Evelyn. 'Bath and London can be very tempting to fashion conscious young ladies. Lots of assemblies, concerts, dinner parties and so many excellent shops.'

Evelyn eyes looked straight at him as she gave him her response, causing him to feel untold longing for her. 'I'm glad that such busy establishments do not tempt me. I love the countryside too much.' She smiled at the captain. 'But it sounds as if there are plenty of social events for us all to enjoy here.'

'The captain has promised us an evening of lively music and dancing at his Seaforth ball,' Primrose said, sounding overjoyed.

'When is the ball? I hope we won't have too long to wait,' said Evelyn, smiling at the captain.

'Could you suggest a suitable date?' he asked her. He would accommodate any date she wanted.

'As long as it is soon, I shall be there,' Evelyn assured him, not realising the effect she had on him.

'It shall be soon,' he promised.

'Was the Heather Park ball a success?' Mr. Ashby asked them. 'It was in full flow when we had to leave for Bath.'

'Heather Park ball was a resounding success,' Mrs. Ashby told her husband. 'And look at the new friends we've made from meeting there.'

Smiles were exchanged around the dinner table.

'I met Mr. Sabastien Hunter in Bath,' Evelyn told them.

'Was he there on business or pleasure?' Captain DeGrey asked sharply, then smiled, refusing to feel jealous of Mr. Hunter.

'Both,' Evelyn replied. 'He attended some social evenings with us, and joined my aunt and me as we went shopping. Then he went to London. He still has his house there, and plans to divide his time between his townhouse in London and Heather Park. Apparently, he has a deep love for London and will always prefer it to Heather Park.'

Captain DeGrey gave his opinion. 'My impression of Mr. Hunter was of a gentleman doing his duty, taking on the responsibility of the Heather Park estate, the inheritance. He seems a city type rather than a country fellow.'

Evelyn nodded. 'Your impression is accurate.'

Mrs. Ashby picked up on Evelyn's tone, the tinge of sadness hidden behind her cheerful smile. Her daughter's heart wasn't broken. But she'd certainly been affected by the company of Mr. Hunter.

'Rupert Feingold played host at Heather Park very well, I thought,' said Mr. Midwinter. 'He's a likeable sort. Very pleasant.'

'Mr. Feingold was so kind to me when he came to Blackhall after the duel,' Miss Midwinter unintentionally said, revealing a hint of what had happened.

Evelyn blinked. 'What duel?' She looked immediately at Captain DeGrey for an explanation.

'I was not involved in the duel,' Captain DeGrey told her.

'No, it was between me and Gilles London,' said Mr. Midwinter.

'Crispin's arm was slashed by Mr. London's sword,' Miss Midwinter added.

Evelyn and Mr. Ashby were both surprised.

'You fought a duel, with swords, with Gilles London?' Mr. Ashby said to Mr. Midwinter.

'I did, but the matter was settled. Gilles London has left and gone back to Bath.'

Miss Midwinter threw in some details now that she was feeling stronger and capable of talking about it. 'Crispin suffered a single wound to his forearm. But Mr. London was cut on his arm, shoulder and chest. He accepted defeat before one of them was badly injured.'

Evelyn was amazed to hear this. She'd imagined everyone would've had a restful time while she was busy in Bath.

Mrs. Ashby thought she may as well add the other details. 'Unfortunately, Charmaine was overcome by the awful event, and feeling weak from lack of sleep and proper nourishment, and the stress of seeing the sword fight, she fainted at Blackhall. Rupert Feingold caught her in his arms and saved her from a harsh fall.'

'How extraordinary,' remarked Mr. Ashby.

'We were going to tell you tomorrow,' said Mrs. Ashby. 'We didn't want to spoil our pleasant evening.'

Mr. Ashby nodded.

The gossip and chatter flowed freely now around the dinner table as they tucked into their meal.

Evelyn spoke to Captain DeGrey. 'So you weren't hurt or involved in the duel?'

'No, I wasn't. I went to Blackhall when I heard about the duel, but it was over and settled by then.'

'Why was there a duel between Mr. Midwinter and Gilles London?' she whispered. 'Was it due to Mr. London's reputation as a charlatan, fooling ladies into believing he truly cares about them?'

The captain nodded. 'Mr. London tried to fool Miss Midwinter. But her cousin put a stop to the trouble by challenging him to a duel.'

Evelyn took a deep breath. 'I'm astonished, but glad that the matter is dealt with.'

CHAPTER TEN

Backgammon was played after dinner. The parlour resounded with laughter and chatter, and gave Evelyn the chance to see the playful side of Captain DeGrey. His company was both entertaining and exciting, and she found herself wishing that the night could last longer.

'I think I must now leave before Mr. Ashby beats me again at this game,' Captain DeGrey said, standing up and smiling.

Mr. Ashby laughed.

'I agree,' Mr. Midwinter chimed–in, getting up from his chair where he was seated beside Annabel. 'I used to believe I was rather good at backgammon, but now having taken a repeated thrashing from Mr. Ashby I shall have to revise my thinking.'

Laughter resounded throughout the company, and the convivial atmosphere continued as the guests got ready to leave.

Miss Midwinter approached Mrs. Ashby. 'Thank you for your kindness and your happy company.'

'Remember, you are always very welcome to join us for sewing,' Mrs. Ashby said, extending an open invitation that was gratefully received.

'And you must come over for tea at Blackhall,' said Miss Midwinter. 'We shall arrange something soon.'

Mr. Midwinter had arrived by carriage, and he drove off home to Blackhall with Charmaine waving out the window to the Ashby family as they stood outside their house. Lanterns lit the doorway of the house, and the windows glowed with candlelight. A night breeze blew through the trees, but they stood there waving off their guests before going inside and getting ready for bed.

Evelyn was the last to go in, preferring to watch Captain DeGrey ride off on his horse. The feelings that stirred inside her would no doubt fill her dreams, that's if she could sleep for the excitement.

From the open window of the study Evelyn heard her father cheer. She smiled to herself, realising her mother must've shown him that while he was away in Bath she'd had the watercolour framed as a welcome surprise. Evelyn's painting of his favourite view now hung on his study wall where he could admire it to his heart's content.

Captain DeGrey rode his horse into the night, heading for Seaforth. The scent of the sea air increased as he charged through the shadows of the countryside, riding faster and faster as his heart was elated. Evelyn Ashby was his heart's desire, and now, after all these years of yearning, her smiles and laughter gave him hope to believe she liked him.

Lit by the glow of moonlight streaming through the branches of the trees, he galloped at speed until the sea was in sight. The water shimmered like dark silver under the midnight sky and the silhouette of Seaforth mansion commanded all it surveyed.

He couldn't help but smile as his heart filled with joy. He stopped for nothing, not even when the force of the wind sweeping past him blew his hat away. It was lost and left behind wherever it had fallen, for he didn't care to stop, riding like the wind with his coat flapping, feeling like his world was about to change for the better, that his life had taken wings.

'Charmaine!' Crispin Midwinter called to her from the main hallway in Blackhall.

She turned to look down at him as she climbed the stairs to retire to her bedroom after their night at the Ashby house.

'Thank you.'

'What for, Crispin?'

'I have not thanked you properly, and for that I apologise, but I shall do it now. Thank you for coming with me to Blackhall. For leaving your life in Oxfordshire behind without complaint or need to be cajoled. Without you here, I would not have endured it on my own. I am grateful, Charmaine, for your company.'

'You are sincerely welcome, Crispin.' She smiled at him, and he smiled back at her, an understanding between them of what a strong bond of friendship they had, and always had. 'See you in the morning.'

He nodded, assured of this. Charmaine was the only constant in his life, but he hoped one day that Annabel Ashby would join her in that accolade.

Captain DeGrey sat in the study at Seaforth. A hundred years of naval ancestry decorated the walls with emblems and artwork. Maps of the ancient world were framed and hung above the large fireplace, and beside a ships compass rescued from a ship belonging to a bygone era — a maritime masterpiece in its own right.

A ubiquitous model of a sailing ship perched on a shelf alongside heavyweight books about the vast oceans and the adventurers that sailed upon them.

Waves crashing against the hull of a magnificent ship as it fought through a storm were captured in an oil painting, in a gilt frame, on the wall adjacent the sturdy desk. No calm sea images were to be found in this study, for it heralded the intrepid admirals and valorous navy captains that had called Seaforth their home.

An anchor, tethered by its own enormous weight, sat in the garden outside the study's window. The chain alone was as thick as an ancient oak. Immovable, it anchored the mood of Seaforth to all who visited, as this was where the carriages were set to stop beside the front lawn.

Anyone with a frivolous mind to change the attitude of the estate's owners had a task as mighty as the sea's tides to alter.

Captain DeGrey was the last link in a long line of seafaring gentlemen guarding Seaforth, ensuring it retained its elegance and history without bowing to fashion or fancy. He found it an honour and would not be the weak link in its continued success.

Barrels of rum from ship's holds had been used to build the bookshelves. The captain, working during the late hours in the night sensed the aroma of the rum, even though it had undoubtedly faded beyond average perception.

By family expectation and obligation, a career in the navy had probably elected him, but he could not have imagined a better choice for himself. Though now, hoping to settle down, he had other plans for his future.

After the exhilarating time he'd had that evening, he was keen to write down all the things Evelyn and her sisters wanted for the ball. He sat alone by candlelight, dipping his quill in ink, and writing a list of the aspects he wanted to include for them.

It was the depths of night, but he couldn't settle, eager to list the dances they loved, the popular songs, and the food. In the morning, he planned to push ahead with the ball and send out the invitations to guests. No hesitation this time.

The Ashby family and the Midwinters knew they'd been invited and the ladies were intending to get their dresses ready.

With the list complete, he headed to bed to get some sleep before the dawn rose.

He blew out one candle in the study and carried the other upstairs to his bedroom.

Moonlight and the shimmer from the sea reflected into his room, casting shadows and shards of light on the walls.

He stripped his clothes off and went to bed, lying there awake thinking of Evelyn smiling at him, joking with him, playing games in the parlour and laughing when they chatted. Of all the things in the world he'd give up everything for, it was her. Only her.

The candle still burned in Evelyn and Annabel's bedroom long into the night.

Snuggled up in their beds, they continued to chatter and gossip.

'I think mama will get her wish this summer,' said Evelyn.

'What? That at least one of us will be engaged to be married before the summer season is over?'

Evelyn hugged the quilt around her and nodded over at Annabel.

'I'm sure Captain DeGrey will propose to you during the ball at Seaforth,' Annabel told her.

Evelyn blinked and laughed. 'I was meaning you. Crispin Midwinter is completely enamoured with you.'

'But it's so sudden. I've barely had time to think, let alone imagine that Mr. Midwinter is so completely taken with me that he would offer me his hand in marriage.'

'Nonsense. We've seen plenty of engagements in the neighbourhood between less acquainted couples. Falling in love is not like a timepiece. If Mr. Midwinter has fallen in love with you, his love will only deepen during the summer.'

'The same could be said of you're attachment to the captain.'

'No, I feel it's different. Unless I am mistaken, Captain DeGrey has been my secret admirer for years.'

Annabel smiled over at Evelyn. 'I think that's so romantic.'

'So do I, but...'

'But what?' Annabel asked, encouraging her to reveal what troubled her.

'Only recently in Bath I was sure I had feelings for Sabastien Hunter. But then he crushed my hopes of a settled life with him, if we were to become attached. He loves London. I don't care for the city. I fear he would never settle in Heather Park even if he found a suitable partner to share it with.'

'You judge him and yourself very harshly.'

'I need to. Convincing myself otherwise would be silly. I was flattered by his attentions, and he is in all other respects handsome and pleasant company, but...'

'He'll never settle down in Heather Park.'

Evelyn nodded over at her sister. 'And that would never work.' She sighed and then spoke of something else that irked her. 'He hid his intentions and plans several times. Even when he was in my company and it would have been mannerly to tell me he was, for example, leaving for London when we were enjoying an evening in Bath. I'd expected to see him the following day. I don't think he noticed my disappointment. He was too taken with the prospect of heading to London.'

'Then it is fortunate you did go to Bath so that Mr. Hunter's character could reveal itself to be incompatible with yours.'

'You're right. But am I wrong to set my hopes on the captain?'

'You're not inclined to be fickle, Evelyn.'

Annabel's assurance calmed her. 'Perhaps I can still take my time to fall in love with him.'

Annabel nodded. 'The summer season is long, and this is only the first flourish of fine sunny days.'

Evelyn laughed lightly. 'The rainstorm was testament to that.'

'So let's plan our dresses for the ball and hope that romance awaits both of us.'

'What about Primrose?' Evelyn asked, feeling disappointed for her.

'You've seen the way gentlemen admire her. She's young. Love will find her I'm sure.'

Evelyn glanced out the window. The dawn was pending. 'We should get some sleep.'

Annabel nodded and snuggled down to sleep.

Evelyn blew out the candle and lay for a moment watching the smoke plume filter into the air, remembering blowing out the candle in Bath, and was now glad that she was home again.

If love could be bottled, Evelyn thought, she imagined it would look like sunbeams in a jar, bouncing around, filled with energy.

And if she was a little in love with Captain DeGrey, this would surely account for her eagerness to rise at her usual early hour, eat breakfast and then take a carriage ride to Heather Park.

Despite little sleep, Evelyn didn't feel the least bit tired, and was on her way to see Raine Feingold, and hoped they could enjoy the day painting outdoors as planned. She'd taken her sketchbook and watercolour paints with her.

She knew that Sabastien Hunter was still in London so she was safe to visit without seeing him. Tilsy's sister worked as one of the Heather Park staff, and had told Tilsy that Mr. Hunter had extended his trip to London. Tilsy then told Mrs. Ashby and Evelyn at breakfast.

Evelyn gazed out the carriage window, looking forward to seeing Raine Feingold.

But when Evelyn arrived at Heather Park staff informed her that Raine Feingold had gone with Rupert Feingold to visit the Midwinters at Blackhall.

Disappointed but not deterred from delighting in a day's painting on such a lovely summer morning, Evelyn travelled home in the carriage, and then walked to the coast. There was a cove where she sometimes sat to paint the sea and coastal flora. No one ever disturbed her there, and it was a fair distance from the Seaforth mansion, so she wouldn't be intruding upon the captain.

Determined to do this, Evelyn headed along the top of the grass edged cliffs towards the cove in the distance. The air was warm and fresh and she breathed it in, feeling it was the tonic she needed.

Captain DeGrey's great grandfather was the first to use the diving point at Seaforth. High above the sea, it provided an ideal spot for private diving and swimming. Mainly diving, and it took a bit of daring to make the dive. The water there was deep, and the cove was shielded against the strong force of the sea that washed up on the rocks. There were no rocks near the diving area. No danger of being washed ashore and ripped to pieces. It was the perfect diving point.

Captain DeGrey stood on the top, stripped to the waist, wearing only beige breeches.

He'd hardly slept, but awoke with excess energy that he needed to work off before setting about his day.

During his time spent sailing in the navy, he'd dived off the decks of the ships into tropical waters. Along with other crew members, he made daring dives for the fun of it.

Standing tall, he looked at the sea, glanced at the water below, and then made the dive.

The water felt great, and he swam up to the surface, exhilarated, then headed back to the shore.

Dripping with sea water, he swept his soaking wet dark hair back from his face and stopped when he heard a woman gasp.

'Captain!' Evelyn said, sounding utterly shocked to see him striding towards her in a state of undress.

'Miss Ashby. I didn't know you were here.'

Evelyn tried to look away, to avoid embarrassing him and herself, but her gaze was drawn to his lean, masculine build. Her heart fluttered and the blush rose in her cheeks.

He had nothing with him to hide his soaking wet appearance, and could only apologise for embarrassing her. 'I'm sorry. I thought I was alone here.'

'I sometimes come here to the cove to paint,' she explained, trying not to peek at him. The beige fabric of his breeches clung to every part of his lower body, emphasising the manly strength of his thighs.

Trying to look as if she wasn't affected by him, she smiled tightly, and hurried away.

'Miss Ashby,' he called after her.

She stopped and glanced back. 'Yes, Captain?'

'May I invite you to have tea with me before you leave? I shall walk behind you and get dressed quickly when we arrive at Seaforth.'

The urgency of his offer made her accept with equal swiftness. It seemed as if they were both eager to rectify the situation and set their friendship again on an even keel.

With the captain striding behind her, Evelyn walked up the grassy path to the top of the cliffs and then on towards Seaforth mansion.

Captain DeGrey disappeared into one of the rooms while a member of staff attended to Evelyn.

She was led into the drawing room. The sun shone in through the windows and the air was warm and welcoming.

'My apologies again,' Captain DeGrey said, striding in wearing dark trousers, a white shirt with cravat, waistcoat and tailcoat. He buttoned up the tailcoat as he walked towards her.

She noticed that his hair was still wet and although he'd swept it back from his face, it refused to be completely smooth, and stray strands dripped across his brow.

In the sunlight, his green eyes made her heart ache just looking at him. If he sensed her feelings, he did not show it. He appeared to be anxious to calm the situation.

As tea was served and they sat down opposite each other, the situation was calm. But Evelyn certainly wasn't. The stirrings in her heart were loud and clear. She was falling in love with him, and there was nothing she could do to prevent it. Not that she wanted to, but she'd never felt this way before about any man, and the strength of the attraction was palpable.

'I was hoping to plan the last aspects of the ball today,' he told her. 'Organise the food and the order of the dances.'

'I'm looking forward to the ball,' she said, and then sipped her tea.

Both of them were conversing politely, while feeling the strong attraction.

'I had a very pleasant evening last night,' he remarked.

'So did I,' she agreed.

'Do you often paint outdoors in the mornings?' he asked.

'I do. The light is ideal at that time of the day. I'd been to Heather Park to see Raine Feingold. We're planning to paint together. But she'd gone to Blackhall with her cousin to visit the Midwinters.'

'So you decided to then come here to paint?'

'I did. It seemed a pity to waste the day.'

He nodded. 'I do not wish to spoil your plans.'

She stood up. 'Perhaps it would be better if I left now.'

Two members of staff had stood in attendance in the drawing room to ensure her reputation wasn't jeopardised. She hadn't been alone with the captain. This wouldn't have been proper, and he was determined not to put her in a vulnerable position.

Captain DeGrey escorted her to the door. They stood in the sunlight for a moment.

'I would be happy to give you a tour of Seaforth some other time, maybe when you're with your sisters or Mrs. Ashby,' he called to her.

'Thank you, I'd like that,' she said, and then continued to walk away.

He watched her leave and wondered what his life would be like if she lived here with him, as his wife. How perfect that seemed.

CHAPTER ELEVEN

The decorative purple plumage in Raine Feingold's fashionable hat outshone those on the hawk.

The bird was being trained by Crispin Midwinter outside Blackhall. He wore a protective leather gauntlet and the hawk perched on his hand.

Rupert Feingold was fascinated by the bird, and while the two gentlemen amused themselves with the hawk training, Raine Feingold and Charmaine Midwinter walked along in the sunshine beside the lake. The water was dark, but so calm they could see their reflections in its glass like surface. The London styling of Miss Feingold's dress and cropped velvet jacket was the height of fashion. Miss Midwinter's dress had a high waistline, short puffed sleeves and the hem was trimmed with ribbon. The lighter fabric suited the summer's day.

'I do admire your dress,' Miss Feingold remarked.

'Sewing with Mrs. Ashby and her daughters put me in the notion of wearing something lighter, less decadent and more suitable for a summer's day. Mrs. Ashby is astoundingly adept at dressmaking and all forms of needlework, and her skills have been passed on to her daughters. Now I'm keen to learn from them. You should join us for sewing. I'm certain they'd love to have your company.'

'I would like to improve my sewing skills, and would indeed care to join you.' Miss Feingold's enthusiasm was clear.

They smiled happily at each other that they had an assured agreement to sew with the Ashby ladies at Heathfield.

Miss Feingold admired her surroundings as she strolled with Miss Midwinter. 'This is a beautiful estate. I hope we haven't disturbed your day, but Rupert had promised to visit you to ensure you'd recovered from the trauma of the duel.'

'You're not disturbing us. We were talking about making changes to the decor at Blackhall. It's far too gloomy and we want to make it more open and lighter in time for the ball.'

They heard the men's laughter far behind them from up on the lawns.

Miss Feingold smiled when she saw Rupert now wearing the gauntlet and attempting to make the hawk do as he commanded. The bird clearly had no intention of doing what Rupert told it. In a flurry of determination, it took off, flying high and then swooping down.

For a moment Miss Feingold walked on, linking arms with Miss Midwinter. But she then realised that the hawk had set its sights on her.

The hawk swooped at speed, attracted by the feathers fluttering in Miss Feingold's hat as she walked. The movement was enough to cause the hawk's instincts to fly straight at her.

Panicking, the women ran screaming, terrified the hawk was attacking them and would claw or peck their faces.

In her haste to run away, Miss Feingold tripped and stumbled into the lake. The weight of her clothes, the long dress and jacket, pulled her under the surface. She fought to swim to the surface, but the weight kept dragging her down, becoming heavier as the layers of fabric were soaked with water.

The day was warm, but the Blackhall lake was never anything except cold and dark. There were times when even Miss Midwinter looked at the lake and shivered as she walked along the edge.

The screams alerted the gentlemen and they came running to help.

Miss Midwinter stood at the edge of the lake and reached out trying to grab hold of Raine Feingold's hand. In desperation she leaned too far and fell into the lake herself.

The women's screams were silenced as they both sank into the depths of the lake.

The gentlemen raced down to the lake, tearing their tailcoats and waistcoats off as they ran full pelt, kicking off their boots.

Racing side by side they both reached the lake at the same time, and without hesitation from either of them, they dived into the lake to save the ladies.

Mr. Feingold was the first to reach Miss Midwinter. He grasped her in one arm and swam with her to the edge of the lake. He lifted her up and placed her safely on the grass. Her breathing assured him she would be fine if he could remove some of her clothes, those that were restricting her breaths due to the fabric tightening around her waist. He pulled at her dress, ripping the stitching on the ties that secured the high waist, but without revealing anything. Her modesty was assured.

Meanwhile, Mr. Midwinter dived repeatedly, searching for Miss Feingold. On his final dive he found her and pulled her seemingly lifeless body to the edge of the lake.

Mr. Feingold helped him lift her out of the water.

'She's not breathing,' Mr. Midwinter uttered. 'Fetch a physician!' he shouted urgently to one of the staff who'd hurried to assist.

The man ran off to get help, but the gentlemen knew the help would be too late to save Miss Feingold.

Mr. Feingold felt the tears run down his face as he shook her and shouted, 'Raine! Come on, Raine! Breath!'

His voice got through to her, and the woman he knew, though outwardly fragile, had an inner strength that few realised. He knew his cousin well and hoped she'd fight to survive.

And she did. She coughed up a mouthful of water, and then gasped for air.

The relief washed over the gentlemen, as they lifted the ladies and carried them back to Blackhall.

Miss Midwinter was safe in the arms of Rupert Feingold, while Miss Feingold was carried by Mr. Midwinter.

Mr. Feingold nodded his reassurance to Miss Midwinter as he carried her with ease, being far stronger than his affable character was perceived. She'd wrapped her arms around his neck and held on tight, glad to be in such capable hands.

The muscles in Mr. Midwinter's jaw twitched with rage, angry at himself for being so negligent with the hawk. A tragedy had been narrowly missed, and he bore the full responsibility of it. He glanced down at Miss Feingold as she rested her head on his shoulder as he carried her towards the house. Her face was pale, and it tortured him that she'd come to Blackhall for unselfish reasons — to enquire about Charmaine. Her kindness had been horribly repaid by his foolish neglect of sense. He should never have put the hawk in Rupert Feingold's charge. It was his responsibility. He blamed no one but himself.

Staff came hurrying to assist them. A physician was on his way, but two of the women staff quickly removed the ladies' wet clothes and put them to bed. Fires were lit to give them heat and warm drinks were offered.

By the time the physician arrived, they were recovering, and he believed they would recover fully after some rest and care.

Rupert Feingold wore dry clothes borrowed from Mr. Midwinter while his own clothes were cleaned and dried by Blackhall staff.

Crispin Midwinter sat glowering at the firelight in the drawing room, wearing a change of clothes, and wishing he'd done things differently.

'Don't blame yourself,' Mr. Feingold told him. 'The ladies are fine.'

He ran a hand through his hair, pushing the wayward dark curls back from his troubled brow. 'I am the only one to blame. But I thank you for helping to save Charmaine. I will be forever indebted.'

'There is no debt or favours needed,' Mr. Feingold told him. 'I'm glad that the ladies are unharmed. Rest will surely right any residue of shock they endure, but I know my cousin well, and she is made of stauncher fabric than her appearance would suggest.'

'Charmaine is the strongest and most capable young woman of my acquaintance, but I feel torn apart that she's had to endure so many recent troubles. I would wish better for her.'

'We both would. So I suggest we pick ourselves up and not burden either of them with our melancholy. That's the last thing they need.'

Mr. Midwinter welcomed Mr. Feingold's suggestion. 'You have my word that I will disguise my disappointment in myself and rally to their recovery.'

'Do not disguise it, Crispin. Cast it aside. Don't let it fester in your thoughts. Your good nature should not be marred by this.'

Mr. Midwinter nodded firmly. A gentlemen's agreement. He admired Mr. Feingold's cheerful smiles, but now understood him rather better. His happy character was true and strong. Sabastien Hunter was fortunate to have Rupert Feingold as his friend.

Primrose stood on a chair while Mrs. Ashby measured the hem of the new lemon dress that Primrose was going to wear to the Seaforth ball.

Annabel was stitching her pale pink dress under the instruction of her mother to sew approximately twelve stitches to an inch along the seams. Mrs. Ashby had cut the pattern pieces and now Annabel was sewing the seams together.

Evelyn intended wearing the lilac dress to the ball, but had cut a dress for herself using the blue fabric from Bath. The colour reminded her of the lightest shade of the sea. Thinking of the sea made her dwell on Captain DeGrey and how wonderful he'd looked when he'd been diving off the coast. The incident had been embarrassing, and yet, it stirred her in ways she found hard to convey without sounding as if she was bubbling with joy having encountered him. Annabel had giggled at the mention of it, and Primrose thought it was very exciting.

Overhearing part of their conversation, Mr. Ashby revealed that he'd dived off the coast into the sea in his younger years and found it quite invigorating.

Mrs. Ashby loved that after all this time she was still finding out little pieces of his past before they'd met. It made her love him all the more.

The trimmings and other items Evelyn had brought back from Bath were shared between all of them, and Mrs. Ashby was especially delighted with the lovely lace trim.

They were all happily sewing away when Tilsy hurried in and quickly whispered the news of the lake incident to Mrs. Ashby.

'Oh, that's dreadful,' Mrs. Ashby said, frowning. 'Are you sure Miss Midwinter and Miss Feingold are unhurt?'

'Yes, ma'am. Apparently Mr. Midwinter dived in and saved Miss Feingold, while Mr. Feingold dived in and saved Miss Midwinter. They each saved the other gentleman's cousin.'

'Do they require our assistance?' Mr. Ashby asked Tilsy.

'No, I don't believe so, sir,' said Tilsy.

'We should call upon them immediately,' Mrs. Ashby said, bustling around the parlour. 'Come on girls, hurry up. Bring your sewing with you.'

Annabel frowned. 'Our sewing?'

'Yes, if the ladies are shocked from almost drowning in the lake, amusement will lift their spirits,' Mrs. Ashby advised. 'Take your dresses with you,' she added, helping Primrose to step out of her lemon dress. 'Fashion and frivolity is what they need. Trust me, I have long experience of such matters.'

And so bags were packed with sewing, half finished dresses, embroidery and bonnets needing trimmed.

Mr. Ashby offered to accompany them, but Mrs. Ashby assured him there was no need, and that he should attend to his business in the study until they came home later in the evening.

The arrival of the Mrs. Ashby and her daughters at Blackhall sparked lively conversation and lifted the mood of Miss Midwinter and Miss Feingold. They were sharing one of the large bedrooms, each of them propped up with pillows in separate beds, but were company for each other. They'd been relaxing when the flurry of their friends burst into the bedroom, laden with sewing bags and cheerful chatter. Sympathies were conveyed regarding the incident at the lake, but then a lively mood filled the room.

'We brought our sewing with us,' Mrs. Ashby told them. 'We thought you'd like to see the dresses we're making and perhaps partake in some embroidery to pass the hours.'

Primrose and Annabel were already unpacking their dresses to show them the progress they'd made. Evelyn unwrapped the pattern pieces she'd cut to make the blue dress.

'I've never seen a dress in the making from a pattern,' Miss Feingold said, taking a keen interest in Evelyn's dressmaking.

Evelyn went over to Miss Feingold's bedside and handed her the pieces. 'I've cut them from one of my mama's patterns. It's a lovely design and easier to sew than you may think. I plan to embroider flowers around the neckline.'

'I like to embroider, but have my dresses made for me in London,' Miss Feingold told Evelyn. 'But I'd love to make my own, or at least try to be involved in the process. The blue fabric is beautiful.'

'I brought some beautiful fabric back from Bath. When you're feeling well enough, come over and spend the day making a dress.'

'Oh, that would be wonderful. I do love fashion and dresses,' Miss Feingold enthused.

Meanwhile, Primrose and Annabel had stepped into the dresses they were making for the ball.

Primrose stood near Miss Midwinter's bedside, where Miss Feingold could view as well, while Mrs. Ashby showed how she'd designed the waistline and the seams.

'That's such a pretty dress,' said Miss Midwinter. 'The pale lemon fabric suits you so well, Primrose.'

Primrose smiled at her. 'The fabric draper's shop has a lovely selection of fabric. If you'd like to make one, you could buy fabric from them and we'd help you make a wonderful dress.'

Miss Midwinter propped herself up higher on her pillows, forgetting about her recent trauma, and smiled with enthusiasm. 'Do you think I'd suit lemon or blue, or pink like Annabel's dress?'

Annabel twirled around to let them see her pastel pink dress. 'Any pastel colours would suit you. You're welcome to try my dress on to see if pink flatters your complexion.'

'Could I?' Without waiting for a reply, Miss Midwinter climbed out of bed and was excited to try on Annabel's dress.

Mr. Midwinter called at the bedroom door, but Mrs. Ashby prevented him from entering. 'The ladies are in a state of undress. We're trying on dresses for the ball and discussing patterns.'

He'd heard the laughter and giggles as he'd walked up the stairs and was pleased that the ladies had brought such joy with them. 'I understand, and shall not disturb you.'

As he went to walk away, Mr. Feingold came hurrying up the stairs. 'Is everything well?' he asked anxiously, hearing the commotion. The two ladies had been resting quietly until their visitors had arrived.

'Our cousins are in fine spirits and feeling better already,' Mr. Midwinter said, smiling.

'Good,' Mr. Feingold said relieved. 'The physician recommended that merriment would help prevent delayed shock,' he confided to Mrs. Ashby. 'I can think of no better ladies to deliver that than yourselves. I am most grateful.'

Mrs. Ashby nodded her assurance to both gentlemen. 'We'll look after your cousins. The day will pass, and tomorrow they will be a lot better I'm sure.'

Nodding and smiling gratefully to Mrs. Ashby, the gentlemen went back downstairs. She heard Mr. Midwinter ask Mr. Feingold if he'd care for a game of cards, and heard his suggestion accepted.

With the men feeling relieved that the ladies were on the mend, the atmosphere at Blackhall lifted. There was happy chaos in the bedroom, but the amount of giggles and gossip shared proved to be the perfect tonic for everyone.

Evelyn was helping Miss Feingold select thread for a floral embroidery when a horse was heard galloping towards the house. Evelyn looked out the bedroom window. 'Captain DeGrey has arrived.'

'He's probably heard about what happened and come to offer his support,' said Mrs. Ashby. And she was right, but he too was soon assured that the ladies were fine and in the capable company of their friends.

Captain DeGrey was given tea and joined in the card games with the gentlemen.

While the Ashby ladies were seated dressmaking, Miss Feingold and Miss Midwinter sat up on their beds embroidering flowers. Evelyn had brought ample thread and pieces of white linen and they used her embroidery patterns to stitch the designs.

'I adore these floral embroidery patterns,' said Miss Feingold to Evelyn. 'Your artistic accomplishments are enviable. I hope you come to Heather Park soon to join me in painting.'

'I shall,' Evelyn replied. 'I'd called at Heather Park earlier today and been told that you were visiting Blackhall. I'd brought my watercolours with me. So, yes, let's paint there soon. I believe Mr. Hunter is still in London.'

'He is,' Miss Feingold confirmed. 'He told Rupert that he was only planning on a short trip to Bath and London, but it seems he has found pleasure in London that keeps him from us.' There was a hint of disappointment in her voice.

'Mr. Hunter seems to enjoy London far more than Heather Park,' said Evelyn. 'I suppose it will be difficult for him to settle down here in the countryside.'

Miss Feingold spoke in a confiding tone. 'That is our concern. Rupert and I were happy to accompany Sabastien to Heather Park and stay for the summer. But it seems that we are to spend more time there without him.'

Mrs. Ashby overheard. 'That's not very thoughtful of Mr. Hunter. The inheritance of Heather Park is his concern. You came to give him company in his new life, and now he's living in London while you take care of the estate.' She pursed her lips, and then continued sewing the short sleeves on Primrose's dress.

'Rupert doesn't mind, but I mind for him.' Miss Feingold sighed. 'The three of us knew we'd miss London. But Rupert says he loves living at Heather Park, and I heartily agree with him. And now we've made such delightful friends. I'm happy to spend the entire summer here.'

Mrs. Ashby stated her opinion clearly. 'Mr. Hunter is the one who is missing out on all the fun and friendship.'

The other ladies nodded.

The sewing continued, as did the card games downstairs. Apart from stopping when afternoon tea and cake was served, the ladies enjoyed a full sewing day at Blackhall.

Miss Feingold looked at the flowers she'd been embroidering. 'I love these pretty blue daisies and bluebells.'

Miss Midwinter had been embroidering flowers too and held up the forget–me–knots she'd been sewing. 'Blue flowers are my favourite, especially forget–me–nots.'

Dinner was served to the ladies in the bedroom, and the three gentlemen came in to take tea with them afterwards.

Rupert Feingold smiled at the two ladies as they sat up in their beds. 'You both look so much better,' he said.

'I feel a lot better, Rupert,' Miss Feingold told him. 'I feel quite fine.'

'So do I,' Miss Midwinter chimed–in, looking bright and happy.

Mr. Midwinter smiled at Charmaine and Miss Feingold. 'I am delighted to hear it.'

This was the first time that evening Captain DeGrey had seen the ladies, and they both looked well. He was pleased for them. He was also delighted to be in the company of Evelyn.

During their tea and cake, light conversation circled between them all, with no further mention of the lake incident.

'Did you enjoy your card games?' Annabel asked Mr. Midwinter.

He smiled and glanced at Captain DeGrey before replying. 'We did, but we were beaten each time by Rupert. Recently, the captain and I were beaten at backgammon by Mr. Ashby. Now it seems we've been beaten at cards by Rupert. We'll have to do better, won't we, Domenic?'

Captain DeGrey nodded and smiled. 'Rupert won every game. I've played some shrewd opponents during my time in the navy, but I tell you, Rupert would've beaten all of them.'

'Rupert's always been good at playing cards,' Miss Feingold told them. 'I've only ever won a handful of games against him, and I suspect he let me win.'

Mr. Feingold simply smiled and let the remarks waft by him. He was rather good at cards, always had been.

'We should set up a game of cards and backgammon between Rupert and Mr. Ashby,' Mr. Midwinter said jokingly. 'I don't know which one I'd bet on to win.'

Mrs. Ashby was sure who'd she'd bet on, and gave a confident smile. 'I would wager that Mr. Ashby would win. He has a mind for numbers the likes of which I've never seen before.'

'In that case, I'll concede to Mr. Ashby,' Mr. Feingold said lightly.

They all laughed and continued to drink their tea.

Mr. Midwinter discussed his plans to brighten up the decor in Blackhall, and this led to the mention of the piano forte in the drawing room.

'Do you play the piano forte?' Mr. Feingold asked Miss Midwinter.

'No,' she replied. 'Sadly, I don't play at all, but I do love listening to others play.'

'Raine plays excellently,' Mr. Feingold said, praising his cousin's ability. 'She's often asked to play during assemblies and dinners in London, for friends of course.'

'When you're well I do hope you'll play for us,' said Miss Midwinter.

Raine loved to play and perked up at the thought of it. 'I feel well enough to play a handful of songs this evening,' she offered.

'Are you sure you're not too tired?' Mrs. Ashby asked her.

'No, I'm not. I'm quite well to play a little this evening.'

After their tea, the company went downstairs to the drawing room where the fire burned cosily and were entertainment by Miss Feingold's playing.

The songs were popular and lively, and encouraged the others to get up and dance.

'Perhaps you should rest by the fire, Charmaine, and not tire yourself,' Mr. Midwinter whispered to her. She'd danced three times with Rupert Feingold.

'Merriment was prescribed to make me well, and there are few happier activities than dancing,' Miss Midwinter whispered back to him.

Knowing that he could not dissuade Charmaine from dancing, Mr. Midwinter smiled and took delight in the cheerful activity.

Music, laughter and chatter filled the room at Blackhall, and the atmosphere was the lightest it had been in years. Rupert Feingold was delighted to dance with Charmaine, and Crispin Midwinter enjoyed dancing with Annabel.

Mrs. Ashby smiled, seeing the connections forming between them. The captain was enthralled to dance with Evelyn, and it warmed her heart that her daughters looked so happy.

Primrose danced once with Mr. Feingold and with Mr. Midwinter, and had a pleasant evening, as did Mrs. Ashby.

At the end of the evening they all bid each other goodnight. But at Miss Midwinter's invitation, Miss Feingold planned to stay the night at Blackhall.

Rather than head back to Heather Park on his own, Rupert Feingold accepted the extended invitation to stay overnight too. He'd danced several times with Charmaine Midwinter, and felt himself more and more attracted to her classic beauty and good nature. Any extension of being close to her was welcomed. His feelings were reciprocated, and several of them noticed the attraction between Rupert and Charmaine.

'I think we have another couple in the making,' Mrs. Ashby whispered to Evelyn.

Evelyn nodded and smiled at her mother.

At the front entrance to Blackhall, Mr. Midwinter bid Mrs. Ashby and her daughters goodnight.

'Do let us know if there's anything else we can do to help Charmaine and Raine,' she said to Mr. Midwinter.

He took her up on her offer to help. 'Would you be able to spare one of your daughters to stay overnight with Charmaine and Raine, just for one night, to ensure they're fine and well?'

Mrs. Ashby's response was instant. 'Of course. Annabel would be a most suitable companion to them for the night.' She deliberately volunteered Annabel because she could see the connection between her and Mr. Midwinter flourish during the evening and wanted to encourage it.

Her choice was met with a delighted smile from Mr. Midwinter. 'Thank you, Mrs. Ashby.'

Annabel herself was delighted to stay.

Mrs. Ashby left with Evelyn and Primrose. Captain DeGrey rode alongside their carriage. Evelyn looked out the window, admiring him as he rode as their escort. He seemed so strong and capable in the saddle. At one point he glanced over, seeing her watching him. They exchanged a look, and she felt the spark of attraction ignite between them again. She'd felt it throughout the evening at Blackhall, especially when she'd danced with him. He danced well. The captain appeared to do everything well.

Ensuring they arrived safely back at Heathfield, he rode home to Seaforth.

Evelyn lingered outside the house, watching the captain ride off into the night. Her heart ached a little for his company. She had grown closer to him again during the evening at Blackhall.

'You'll see the captain again soon,' Mrs. Ashby assured her. 'The Seaforth ball is only a few days away.'

Smiling at her mother, Evelyn linked arms with her and they headed inside the house.

Evelyn lay in bed watching the candle flicker. She wondered if Annabel had fallen completely in love with Crispin Midwinter, for it was clear to her that he was falling in love with Annabel. They would make a wonderful couple she was sure.

With pleasant thoughts of dancing with Captain DeGrey at Blackhall, and more dancing soon at the Seaforth ball, Evelyn blew the candle out and went to sleep.

CHAPTER TWELVE

A couple of days later, Evelyn travelled in the carriage to Heather Park to spend the day painting in the sunshine with Raine Feingold.

On arrival, a member of the staff relayed news that sent a stab of disappointment through her heart. She'd been looking forward to seeing Raine and had brought her watercolours along with her in the hope that they'd enjoy the day together. She imagined they'd discuss the forthcoming ball at Seaforth and exchange gossip and chatter. Instead she was told that Miss Feingold and Mr. Feingold had gone home to London, and had no plans to return soon, if at all. Neither had Sabastien Hunter. Heather Park was to be shuttered, and furnishings hidden under dust sheets, and left empty except for a handful of staff for the foreseeable future.

Evelyn stood in the sunshine outside the front entrance of Heather Park, and felt chilled from the news. She didn't blame Raine or Rupert Feingold, for she believed them to be thoughtful people, so it could only be the intervention of someone else that had made the decision for them. And that person was surely Sabastien Hunter.

In the carriage ride back home to Heathfield, Evelyn gazed out the window at the bright sunny day, the beautiful countryside and blue sky. The warmth of the day, and the scent of the flowers and greenery, wafted in the carriage window. It felt like the real world was right there, that she could grasp it if she stopped the carriage, and got out and stood in the sunlight. But she knew she wouldn't. Just as she knew there was nothing she could do to bring the Feingolds back to Heather Park, and make their lives bright and filled with summer sun again. They were gone. London was far away. Soon, they would all be but happy memories of each other.

'They've gone home to London?' Mrs. Ashby exclaimed when Evelyn told her the news. Her shrill voice caused Annabel and Primrose to come running into the parlour where Mrs. Ashby was putting the finishing stitches to their dresses for the Seaforth ball.

'What's wrong?' Annabel said, hurrying over to her mother.

Primrose could tell by her mother's disapproving expression that something unpleasant had occurred. 'Has something happened?'

'Raine and Rupert Feingold have gone back to London,' Mrs. Ashby stated, clearly annoyed. 'Without warning. Without concern for the consternation of others in their circle.'

Evelyn explained the details to her sisters, and Mr. Ashby came through from his study to hear what the commotion was about.

There was a stunned silence for a moment as Evelyn told them that Heather Park was being shuttered that morning. 'It was a distressing sight to behold.'

'I thought Raine had arranged to have you call on her this morning at Heather Park to paint together,' Mrs. Ashby said to Evelyn.

'She did. I spoke to her only recently at Blackhall. Raine was fully recovered, and Mr. Feingold was taking her back to Heather Park in the carriage,' Evelyn explained. 'Nothing in her manner led me to believe that she was leaving for London.'

'Why would they keep such plans a secret?' Mrs. Ashby demanded to know.

'Perhaps they had no plans to leave,' Evelyn surmised. 'I suspect Sabastien Hunter is behind their swift decision to vacate Heather Park.'

Mr. Ashby nodded. This made sense to him. 'Sabastien Hunter really never settled here. Maybe he informed them that he wasn't planning to return soon to Heather Park, and this forced the Feingolds to leave. After all, they are his guests. Without the host, the guests would be obliged to leave and go back home.'

The ladies agreed with Mr. Ashby's scenario.

'But it doesn't excuse Raine and Rupert Feingold's behaviour,' Mrs. Ashby insisted. 'It would have been mannerly to tell us in person instead of disappearing into the wind.'

'I would expect a letter from Raine in London soon,' Evelyn said hopefully. 'Then we may understand what happened.' No promise of a letter had been made, but she felt that her friend would surely want to write to her from London.

Mrs. Ashby put her sewing aside and pulled her lace edged shawl around her shoulders, as if she'd been ruffled and needed to straighten herself out. The news didn't sit easily with her. She was mildly insulted on behalf of Evelyn.

'Well,' Mrs. Ashby announced. 'The Feingolds have gone. We have a ball to look forward to. So let's not allow their bad manners to spoil our joy.'

Mr. Ashby went back through to his study while the ladies continued with their dressmaking and embroidery. They were quiet for a short while, busying themselves in their stitching. Evelyn was finishing whitework and goldwork embroidery, but she could barely concentrate on the satin stitching for thinking about the distress that Raine had caused her by leaving.

Tea and lemon cake was served up by Tilsy, and this seemed to lighten the mood.

'Did you hear anything about the Feingolds leaving Heather Park and going home to London?' Mrs. Ashby asked Tilsy.

Tilsy hesitated, indicating she had heard something, but wasn't sure whether to tell Mrs. Ashby.

'Out with it, Tilsy,' Mrs. Ashby encouraged her.

'There's gossip that Mr. Sabastien Hunter gave little notice to his staff at Heather Park that he would not be coming back. He plans to stay in London. Apparently, Mr. Rupert Feingold, a gentleman of pleasant character, as you know, ma'am, became very angry when he received the news.'

'I can't imagine Rupert Feingold being angry,' said Evelyn.

Tilsy nodded. 'The Heather Park staff were very surprised. He was completely enraged that Mr. Hunter had put him and his cousin, Miss Feingold, in such an unfortunate position.'

'That they couldn't stay at Heather Park if Mr. Hunter had no intention of living there?' Evelyn asked Tilsy.

'Yes,' said Tilsy. 'It put them in an awkward position.'

'They surely wouldn't be forced to leave Heather Park with such urgency,' Annabel remarked.

Mrs. Ashby looked ruffled. 'It seems as if they packed their bags in the middle of the night when no one would argue their leaving.'

'They did leave as you suggest, ma'am,' Tilsy agreed. 'Mr. Feingold was angry with Mr. Hunter and wanted to confront him and wouldn't wait until the morning. He had the carriage take them back to London immediately. The staff say, though it is only gossip, that Mr. Feingold was shouting and raging, not at staff, but at Mr. Hunter's selfish decision to forgo his inheritance in favour of residing in London.'

'Thank you for telling us, Tilsy,' said Mrs. Ashby.

Tilsy nodded, and then hurried away, leaving the ladies to churn over the details of the reliable gossip.

'Miss Midwinter will be sorely disappointed. Her attachment to Rupert Feingold was a promising one. He clearly adored her. I had high hopes of them becoming a popular couple.' Mrs. Ashby shook her head. 'Poor Charmaine. She's had one burden after the other to deal with.'

Evelyn felt her friend's distress. 'I fear she'll be completely broken–hearted.'

Charmaine was due to arrive at Heathfield to join them in their sewing.

Primrose looked out the window hearing a carriage arrive. 'Miss Midwinter is here.'

A small carriage pulled up outside the house, driven by Crispin Midwinter. He'd brought Charmaine to enjoy a day's sewing.

Charmaine was welcomed in by Evelyn and Annabel, but she could tell that something was amiss.

They brought her into the parlour and Mrs. Ashby began to explain what had happened.

Mr. Ashby strode outside to speak to Mr. Midwinter before he drove off.

'Crispin. A word with you before you leave,' Mr. Ashby called to him.

Mr. Midwinter jumped down from the carriage. 'Is something wrong?'

Mr. Ashby explained what had happened.

Mr. Midwinter ran a troubled hand through his hair and felt distraught for Charmaine. 'May I impose upon you to keep Charmaine safe while I go to Heather Park to find out all I can about what's happened?' he asked Mr. Ashby.

'Charmaine will be safe with us, and it is no imposition,' Mr. Ashby assured him.

Nodding to Mr. Ashby, he climbed into the carriage and drove with haste to Heather Park. If even half of this news was true, the repercussions, especially to Charmaine, were enormous. He would demand an explanation, and if it did not meet his satisfaction, he would drive forthwith to London to confront Rupert Feingold and Sabastien Hunter in person. Charmaine had endured too many upsets recently for them to add to her distress through their selfishness or folly.

Charmaine sat in the parlour being comforted by Mrs. Ashby and her daughters.

'She's looking very pale,' Annabel whispered to Evelyn.

Mrs. Ashby clasped Charmaine's hand. 'We'll get you a cup of tea and you can stay with us until you feel better,' she assured her.

Charmaine appeared to be in shock, exacerbated by the recent events all being piled on to her.

Mr. Ashby came in and looked at her. He frowned at his wife. 'Crispin has gone directly to Heather Park to find out exactly what has happened,' he said quietly.

Charmaine glanced up at him. 'Are you certain that Mr. Feingold has gone?' There was a glimmer of hope in her wide grey eyes that were threatening to fill up with tears. 'Will he becoming back to Heather Park?'

Mr. Ashby glanced at his wife and shook his head. Then he replied softly. 'Crispin has gone to Heather Park to find out. In the meantime, Mrs. Ashby and the girls will see that you are fine.'

Charmaine nodded but looked incredibly pale.

Evelyn took her father aside. 'I fear it's all been too distressing for her.'

A rider was heard arriving outside the house. Evelyn glanced out the window. 'It's Captain DeGrey.'

'Show the captain in, Tilsy,' said Mr. Ashby.

The captain was in a cheerful mood as he walked into the parlour. He was carrying packages with him. In his enthusiasm, he didn't observe Charmaine's distress, and couldn't wait to gift them the parcels. 'I was passing the linen draper's shop this morning, and I saw they had lots of thread in the window display. You'd mentioned at Blackhall that with all the sewing you ladies had been doing you need to restock on your embroidery thread. I went in, and the shop assistant was familiar with your tastes.' He handed the packages to Evelyn. 'She recommended these threads, so I bought them all hoping they would be of some use to you.'

Evelyn accepted the gift, and under other circumstances her response would've been more openly joyous, but she glanced at

Charmaine and then at the captain, trying to show him that something was amiss.

'Have I called at an inconvenient time?' the captain asked.

'The Feingolds have gone home to London,' Mr. Ashby told him. 'We've only just received the news. It's all been a bit too much for Charmaine. I'm sure you understand.'

'I do,' he said, nodding. He glanced at Evelyn. 'Is there anything I can do to help?'

'Mr. Midwinter has gone to Heather Park to enquire about the predicament,' Evelyn explained. 'Perhaps you could stay for a short while until he returns with news.'

Captain DeGrey surmised he may be needed to ride for help if Miss Midwinter required assistance. She looked remarkably pale. The anger started to build up in him as further details were confided to him by Mr. Ashby and Evelyn.

Tilsy brought tea and biscuits through to the parlour and set them on a table beside Miss Midwinter. A warm shawl was wrapped around her shoulders and logs added to the fire for warmth. Even though the sun was shining, it had yet to heat the parlour.

Charmaine sipped her tea and tried not to be a burden to the Ashby family. 'I will be fine. I was just surprised that Rupert had gone so suddenly. We'd been talking about the ball and Seaforth and he'd made me promise to dance with him all evening.' She smiled tightly at the thought of this. 'Now it seems he will not be in attendance.'

'We'll still have a lovely time,' Mrs. Ashby assured her.

Evelyn sat down beside her. 'You'll be with us, and your cousin and the captain. I'm sure Captain DeGrey has wonderful plans for the ball.'

'I do,' he confirmed. 'Everything is set. The music, the dances and the food is all arranged.'

Charmaine smiled up at him. 'Thank you, captain. It sounds delightful.'

The tea and comforting company help revive Charmaine's spirits and soon the colour was starting to come back into her cheeks.

Evelyn set the selection of thread on the table. 'The captain has bought lots of thread. We can finishing the embroideries we were working on. Or we can help finish the dresses for the ball.'

As more tea was made, and they sat sewing dresses and working on their embroidery, the atmosphere started to ease from the shock of the Feingolds leaving Heather Park.

'I just can't believe that Rupert would be so heartless,' Captain DeGrey confided to Evelyn.

'Apparently, he was angry with Sabastien Hunter and headed straight to London to confront him,' she explained.

'That I can believe,' the captain said. 'If no news is received soon, I shall travel to London personally to make enquires and demand an explanation.'

Evelyn smiled at him. 'Hopefully, it won't be necessary, but I thank you for your support.'

'Do you think I should cancel the ball, or postpone it?' he asked Evelyn.

'No, I do not. Happy events should not be cancelled because of the thoughtlessness of others.'

He nodded firmly.

While they waited for Crispin Midwinter to come back from Heather Park, the ladies busied themselves in their sewing, while the captain took another beating playing cards this time with Mr. Ashby.

Eventually, a carriage drove up and Mr. Midwinter came hurrying in.

'The gossip is true,' he announced, striding into the parlour. 'But there is hope. Rupert Feingold was happy living at Heather Park, as was Miss Feingold. I trust that Mr. Feingold with settle this nonsense with his friend, Mr. Hunter, and come back again soon.'

Charmaine perked up at this and looked hopeful. 'Are you sure?'

'I believe I am a reliable judge of character,' he said. 'Rupert was starting to form an attachment with you, Charmaine, and I do not think he's the type of gentleman to play with your affections lightly.'

She agreed. Rupert Feingold was nothing like Gilles London.

During the remainder of the day, Miss Midwinter remained in the company of the Ashby ladies, sewing and chatting.

Mr. Ashby entertained Mr. Midwinter and Captain DeGrey in his study.

‘I believe the ladies, especially Miss Midwinter, would benefit from our reliable company,’ Mr. Ashby had told the gentlemen. And all of them stayed to have dinner with the family that evening.

No more news had been forthcoming about the Feingolds or what was to become of Heather Park. Despite this, they rallied in each other’s company and were looking forward to the ball at Seaforth.

Before leaving that night Captain DeGrey handed Evelyn a private letter without giving her an explanation of its contents. His green eyes looked intense as he handed her the letter, imploring her to keep the exchange between the two of them.

Evelyn accepted the letter. She tucked it into her sewing box where she kept precious trinkets, private notes and items of sentimental value that to others would be of no worth at all.

The Ashby family gathered at the front entrance to Heathfield and waved their guests goodnight.

Mr. Midwinter drove his carriage away with Charmaine back to Blackhall. She had once again benefited from the capable company of the Ashby ladies. To protect her heart she had settled herself to accept that Rupert Feingold was probably to be part of her past rather than her future.

Captain DeGrey mounted his horse, nodded farewell to the family, and with a knowing glance at Evelyn, he then rode off home under the pale moonlight to Seaforth. They would not meet again until the evening of the ball.

As the family went back inside the house and tidied away their games and embroidery, and got ready for bed, Evelyn slipped the secret letter into her handkerchief and hid it under her pillow.

Tucked up in bed, she fussed with the pleating of her hair, keeping the candle at her bedside alight until Annabel fell asleep. Then she snuggled up and opened the captain’s letter, breaking the red wax seal that ensured no one else had opened it, and read it by the flickering candle’s glow...

Dear Miss Ashby, I am writing to you in the hope that I may make my intentions to you quite clear in the assured privacy of this letter. I have matters to confess that require clarity of purpose, as I fear they may be misconstrued if uttered lightly or with interruption from others.

You cannot have failed to notice my sincere affection for you. However, my affections are more than of recent source. I have loved you, my dear Evelyn, for the past four years. When I first saw you from afar, I fell in love with you then, even before we were introduced. I admired your beauty and pleasant character, and the way you were happy with your family. But I was too young and inexperienced in matters of the heart, and of the world, to express my affections openly. So I left with the intention of coming back when I was ready to offer you everything you deserve for a comfortable, safe and prosperous life. I now believe I am in the fortunate position to offer all these things to you, and I hope that you will do me the honour of dancing the first dance with me at the Seaforth ball, and allow me to stand before you without any secrets between us. I have wanted to tell you, since settling in Seaforth, of my devotion to you, only you, for I have loved no other in the four years I have been away.

If my sentiments meet with your approval, your acceptance of the first dance with me at the ball will confirm that you are willing to let me prove to you that I am capable of making you happy. This would surely make me the happiest gentleman at the ball.

If my intentions are unwelcome, for whatever reason, you need not explain, and I will never utter any mention of this again. I would then hope we could at least be pleasant acquaintances, for I do admire and enjoy the company of your family members.

I look forward to seeing you at the ball, my dearest Evelyn, and finding out if my bold intentions are welcome.

The letter was signed, Captain Domenic DeGrey.

Evelyn wiped away the stray tears of happiness that fell from her eyes as she read the letter. She glanced over at Annabel, but her time reading the letter was as he'd wished — private between only her and the captain.

She folded the letter and slipped it under her pillow for safe keeping until the morning when she intended putting it her sewing box as a precious letter she would not part with.

Blowing out the candle, her heart was filled with hope, joy and love that was surely going to be. For there was nothing that she could imagine to prevent her accepting Captain DeGrey's proposal to dance, and a further proposal to let herself fall completely in love with him without fear of rejection or being broken–hearted.

A letter arrived for Evelyn the next morning. Tilsy handed it to Evelyn as she sat at the dining table having breakfast.

The chatter paused in anticipation that it was news from London, from Raine or Rupert Feingold.

Evelyn put her tea aside, broke the wax seal on the letter and opened it.

'Is it from London?' Mrs. Ashby asked eagerly.

'It is,' Evelyn confirmed, and continued to read it.

'From Raine Feingold?' Mrs. Ashby said hopefully.

Evelyn shook her head and read the message.

'What does Rupert have to say?' Mr. Ashby asked, assuming it was from Mr. Feingold.

'The letter isn't from either of them,' said Evelyn, still reading it and attempting to absorb the message.

'Then who is it from?' Mrs. Ashby demanded, impatient to find out.

Evelyn looked up from the letter. 'It's from Sabastien Hunter.'

Mrs. Ashby frowned and looked as if this was distasteful. 'What does that scoundrel have to say for himself?'

'He says he intended trying to settle at Heather Park, but events in London conspired against him.'

Mrs. Ashby raised her brows in disbelief and exchanged a look with Mr. Ashby.

Annabel and Primrose glanced at each other, but kept quiet while Evelyn read the letter to them...

'Dear Miss Ashby, I am writing to you for two purposes. The first is to apologise for not contacting you after our fortunate time in Bath came to an end when I left for London. My intention in coming to Bath was to meet with you, as I believed us to have made a happy acquaintance with each other at the Heather Park ball. I wished to see you again, and I enjoyed our time in Bath. I was there also to find out the character of Mr. Gilles London, and I do not need to reiterate what a devious man he is.

'Secondly, I'm writing to clarify that I do not foresee myself settling down in the near future at Heather Park. I'm certain the news of this has reached you and is the joy of local gossipmongers. However, I did intend trying to settle myself at Heather Park, but events in London conspired against my true intentions. I was otherwise engaged in business and obligations that would require deep explanation, but you can be assured that these matters were of the utmost necessity, regardless of whatever things you have heard to the contrary.

'This is my personal assurance that I will one day settle at Heather Park, if not entirely, at least for part of the year, with the remainder living in London.

'It is my sincere hope that when we meet again in the future, our friendship would have endured the separation and we shall resume our connection. I plan to marry and settle down, but not for some time as I have many matters that benefit being a single man, and I would not burden a wife with waiting for me without assurance of my company.

'If I may, I would like to write to you sometimes to maintain our acquaintance. If I do not receive a reply to this letter, I will assume my offer has been rejected.'

Evelyn finished reading the letter and sighed heavily.

'Well,' Mr. Ashby said, taking a deep breath. 'That was quite a letter, though it doesn't clarify much of anything.'

Mrs. Ashby disapproved. 'Is Mr. Hunter just going to leave that beautiful house at Heather Park shuttered and under dust sheets until it suits him to come back? If he ever does. I doubt it by the sounds of his flimsy excuses.'

'You're right,' said Evelyn. 'This letter says everything and yet nothing. He makes no attempt to admit that he prefers living in London and that the countryside isn't to his taste.'

'Are you going to keep in touch with him?' Primrose asked Evelyn.

'No.' Evelyn's reply was clear.

'What did he say again about his business and obligations in London?' Annabel said to Evelyn.

'Here, read it.' Evelyn handed the letter to Annabel. 'Perhaps you'll make more sense of it.'

Annabel read it while the conversation continued.

'Mr. Hunter makes no mention of the Feingolds,' Mrs. Ashby complained. 'It's as if they are of no consequence to him.'

'He's a selfish man,' said Mr. Ashby.

'I intend showing the letter to Charmaine and Mr. Midwinter,' Evelyn told them. 'But I doubt it will make either of them feel better about the situation.'

'I would suggest showing it to them this morning,' Mrs. Ashby advised. 'Let them read it, and then let's all try to look forward to the ball. Mr. Hunter isn't even here and he's causing all these ructions.'

Evelyn hurried over to the window when she heard a carriage arriving. 'That's Charmaine and Mr. Midwinter here now.'

Annabel folded the letter and handed it back to Evelyn.

Charmaine smiled as she came in. She'd brought the embroidery she'd been working on with her, along with the dress she planned to wear to the ball. She hoped they'd help advise her on embroidering the neckline.

Mr. Midwinter accompanied Charmaine, but both of them sensed something was wrong.

Evelyn handed the letter to Mr. Midwinter. 'I received this letter from Sabastien Hunter this morning.'

He read it immediately.

Charmaine hurried over to him. 'What does it say?'

He frowned as he continued reading it. 'The letter says nothing about Rupert or Raine Feingold.' He passed the letter to Charmaine.

She read it quickly and then shook her head in dismay. 'Why wouldn't Mr. Hunter even mention them? Rupert was supposed to be his friend.' She gave the letter back to Evelyn.

'Is Heather Park to remain as it is?' Mr. Midwinter asked them.

No one knew.

Mr. Ashby shrugged. 'I fear we are wasting our time looking for answers to things that Mr. Hunter has no intention of clarifying.'

Evelyn handed the letter to her father. 'Please keep this with your letters in the study.'

'Don't you want to keep it in your sewing box?' Mr. Ashby said, knowing she kept all her special items there.

'No, I don't wish to keep it.'

Mr. Ashby took the letter and put it away in his study.

Mr. Midwinter followed him through to have a word with him in private.

'Charmaine was happy to come here to embroider her dress for the ball,' Mr. Midwinter confided. 'She seems so much better and I hope she won't dwell on thoughts of what's happening at Heather Park.'

'Mrs. Ashby will ensure this. The excitement of the ball is just what we all need until this whole sorry business with Mr. Hunter is sorted out.'

CHAPTER THIRTEEN

The windows of the Ashby family house were aglow in the warm summer evening on the night of the Seaforth ball. The carriage, with its lanterns lit, sat ready to drive them there.

The activity inside the house revolved around Mrs. Ashby and her daughters getting dressed in their finery. Mr. Ashby's main fuss was tying his new cravat around the collar of his white shirt so that the bee Evelyn had embroidered showed at the front for all to see. His tailcoat was buttoned over his silk back waistcoat, one of the waistcoats the women had stitched for him. He was feeling smartly dressed and hopeful. Since the letter arrived from Mr. Hunter a few days ago, their lives had settled down again, attending to the things that brought them joy and getting ready to attend the ball.

'Help me tie my sash, mama,' Primrose urged her mother.

Mrs. Ashby stopped fussing with Annabel's pink dress, and tied the satin ribbon sash at the back of Primrose's lemon dress.

She stood back and admired her two youngest daughters and smiled. 'You both look beautiful.'

Evelyn sat in front of the dressing table mirror and pinned a sparkling clasp into her upswept hair. Tiny glittering clips were added here and there making it look like dragonflies were flitting about in her strawberry blonde hair.

'Remember to pin those artificial flowers on your bag,' Evelyn reminded Primrose.

Primrose had forgotten and rushed to find the selection of fabric flowers that included lily of the valley. She pinned them on her bag, and handed Annabel a spray of pink flowers to pin on her bag too.

Evelyn stood up and smoothed her hands down the silky lilac fabric of her dress. The colour was perfect for her. She'd never worn lilac before, and probably wouldn't have considered it had her aunt not given her the dress. To match it, she'd embroidered lilac, lavender, heliotrope and night scented stock flowers on her reticule. The bag was secured with lilac ribbons, and completed the fashionable look of her attire. She'd made it in a pale lilac fabric that was one of the off–cuts from the fabric draper's shop.

'You look beautiful too, Evelyn,' Mrs. Ashby said, smiling at her.

Mr. Ashby knocked on the bedroom door. 'We'd better leave now or we'll be late for the ball.'

With a flurry of last minute checks on their hair, dresses and bags, they hurried out to the carriage to head to the ball.

Excited chatter filled the carriage during the entire ride to Seaforth. Mr. Ashby sat beside the ladies, letting their laughter and talk of romance waft around him.

Evelyn gazed out the window as they approached the coast road. She saw the mansion in the distance. Lights shone from the main rooms and there were torches illuminating the front entrance.

Her heart fluttered at the thought of meeting Captain DeGrey for the first time since she'd received his letter. She hadn't told anyone, not even her sisters, about the letter or its romantic overtures. It was hidden safely in her sewing box. The thought that the captain had loved her for years was almost overwhelming. Almost. For she delighted in the idea that he truly loved her, and that they would form an attachment at the ball that would lead to an engagement perhaps by the end of the summer. Every time she'd been in the captain's company, she felt more drawn to his character, for he was kind and capable and strong. All qualities she admired in a gentleman. She'd never loved deeply, and the frivolous flirtations she'd had since she was seventeen were no more than that — silly notions that sometimes would last for an evening, during a dinner or dance, and then be gone by the morning. She felt her heart's loyalty could be assured if she ever met the right man, and now she had high hopes that she'd met him. Captain DeGrey was everything she could hope for in a partner.

The voices of the guests drifted in the carriage windows as they drove up and stopped outside the front entrance of Seaforth. Music was heard playing in the background, and numerous others were arriving, all dressed in their finery, to enjoy the ball.

Evelyn was reminded of the night at Heather Park when they'd attended the impromptu ball. Little did she know the friends she'd make from there, or the circumstances that led to her being here.

Mr. Ashby helped his wife and daughters alight from the carriage.

Evelyn gazed at the magnificence of the mansion. Different in style and architecture, and with its coastal location, it was as impressive as Heather Park, yet a wonderful venue for a ball in its own right.

Captain DeGrey stood in the main entrance hall greeting his guests.

His back was towards them as they approached, but suddenly he glanced round, as if something compelled him to look over his shoulder. He smiled broadly when he saw Evelyn and her family.

Then the expression on his handsome face became tense, as if he was prepared to have his heart broken if Evelyn refused his proposal of an attachment. But the look she gave him, that stretched between them, as if the world had stopped to accommodate that moment when her look would indicate if he'd spoken out of turn, gave him hope. Evelyn Ashby was prepared to let herself fall in love with him.

Evelyn smiled at Captain DeGrey. This was all the confirmation he needed.

His entire attitude was bolstered, and he breathed deeply, his shoulders feeling broader and lighter from the realisation that Evelyn's heart belonged to him. And only him.

Other fine gentlemen were in attendance, and he'd ensured to invite each guest with a personal invitation. All invitations had been accepted. No one wanted to miss out on the ball, especially as the issue with Heather Park was the talk of the local gossip.

Crispin Midwinter and Charmaine had arrived shortly before the Ashby family, and were admiring the splendour of Seaforth when Mr. Midwinter noticed Annabel. He smiled at her, thinking how lovely she was in her pink dress, and he went over to them accompanied by Charmaine.

Charmaine's dress was a vision in white with embroidery around the neckline. Her dark hair was pinned up, and she was carrying the reticule that Evelyn helped her sew. Tiny beads sparkled on the bag's embroidered flowers and butterflies.

The Midwinters came over to join the Ashby family, and with all the bustling activity at the start of the ball, no one noticed the loving looks the captain gave to Evelyn. He still could hardly believe she liked him.

As the first dance was due to begin, Captain DeGrey held out his hand to Evelyn. She accepted it and smiled, and let him lead her on to the dance floor.

They were joined by numerous couples, including Mr. and Mrs. Ashby.

Octavia Thornbee, unsmiling as usual but looking beautiful, was dancing with a gentleman, while Lady Thornbee chatted to acquaintances.

A gentleman asked Miss Midwinter to dance, and she accepted so as to leave her cousin free to dance with Miss Annabel. It was clear to Charmaine that this was what he wanted, but he wouldn't leave her standing alone while he enjoyed dancing.

Another young gentleman escorted Miss Primrose on to the dance floor, and soon they were all involved in the dancing.

Captain DeGrey smiled at Evelyn and whispered to her when he had a brief moment in the dance. 'I trust you are happy to be here. You look beautiful. I hope I may dance with you for most of the evening.'

Evelyn smiled at him. 'Indeed you may, captain.'

Mrs. Ashby noted to her husband. 'Look at Captain DeGrey smiling at Evelyn. I think an engagement seems promising.'

There was no disguising the romantic attraction between the captain and Evelyn.

Mr. Ashby nodded to his wife and smiled. 'I believe you are right, my dear.'

'And Mr. Midwinter is enthralled with Annabel,' she added, glancing over at them dancing together.

'You did say that you hoped that at least one of our daughters would be engaged before the end of the summer,' he recalled. 'It seems you were right about that too.'

Mrs. Ashby smiled at him. 'Now all we need is someone wonderful for Primrose.'

'Primrose is still young enough to find romance in due course,' said Mr. Ashby. 'Let us delight in the happiness of Evelyn and Annabel for the present.'

Mrs. Ashby nodded and they continued to dance.

Everyone was happy and the atmosphere was cheerful, but it changed in an instant when two figures stood at the entrance to the ballroom awaiting their introduction and welcome from the host.

The music continued to play, but couples faltered in their dancing and guests stared at the unexpected arrival.

'What are they doing here?' Mrs. Ashby said to her husband. Her surprised tone sounded above the music, causing everyone who'd failed to see the late guests look over at them.

Charmaine's heart felt the shock of their arrival. She'd convinced herself that she would not see Rupert Feingold again soon. Or Raine. Now they were standing in the ballroom as if they were part of the merriment. But instead, they caused the dancing to pause by their mere presence.

Captain DeGrey walked over to them, escorting Evelyn with him.

'I apologise that we're late for the ball,' Mr. Feingold said to the captain.

There was an awkwardness that neither of them wanted to disguise.

The captain nodded. 'I didn't expect you to attend the ball this evening.'

'We've been in London, as I suspect you'd heard,' Mr. Feingold stated.

'I did,' the captain said, and then sighed in exasperation. 'What happened, Rupert? You and Raine disappeared without a word to any of us. Charmaine was particularly distressed.'

Rupert looked upset. 'I'm sorry if my leaving caused Charmaine to be upset. It was not my intention. Circumstances warranted I leave for London immediately.'

'I understand that Sabastien Hunter is not coming back to Heather Park,' said Captain DeGrey.

'Not for the foreseeable future, no,' Mr. Feingold confirmed. 'I wonder if I could address you and our other friends with the news I have. Perhaps it would clear any bad feelings we've obviously caused.'

The captain nodded.

By now the other members of the Ashby family, along with the Midwinters, had joined them.

In the background, the dancing continued, but guests were eager to see what was happening.

'What is your news?' said Captain DeGrey encouraging Mr. Feingold.

'When Raine and I left Blackhall that evening we last spoke to you, we received a letter from Sabastien as we arrived at Heather Park. He said he was staying in London and wasn't coming back to Heather Park, and that we should come home to London. I was extremely angry, and insisted we leave immediately to confront my friend in London.'

'You could've told us your plans,' Mr. Midwinter snapped at him.

'I apologise. I was upset for Raine, for the entire situation, and at Sabastien's arrogance that he should treat us without consideration.'

'We do understand that you're upset with us,' Miss Feingold added.

'I only found out you'd gone when I went to paint with you at Heather Park,' Evelyn told her. 'The house was being shuttered, and both you and Rupert had gone without a word to any of us.'

'I'm truly sorry, Evelyn,' Miss Feingold said, sounding upset. 'We were so distressed ourselves that we left that night for London. I was going to write to you, but I was hopeful I could explain to you when we got back here.' She glanced at Rupert. 'I knew that Rupert planned to deal with Sabastien. I thought we would be back soon to explain to you properly.'

They waited for Mr. Feingold to explain.

Rupert Feingold took a deep breath and came right out with it. 'I now own Heather Park. Raine and I are planning to live there now, not London.'

This news surprised them all.

Mr. Ashby wanted clarification. 'You've bought Heather Park, Sabastien Hunter's house and estate?'

Mr. Feingold stood strong. 'That is correct.'

Raine could see the doubt in their expressions, so she added her own clarification. 'Rupert is as wealthy as Sabastien, probably more so. They have come to a mutually suitable financial arrangement. Rupert will take on the inheritance and maintain Heather Park as it should be.'

'What of Mr. Hunter?' Mrs. Ashby asked them.

'We are still acquaintances, friends of sorts,' Mr. Feingold explained. 'But I do not hold him in the same esteem I once did. I favour all of your company far more. However, it is better that Sabastien and I are not enemies, especially as there will be a few matters from time to time regarding Heather Park that will require our civil exchange of conversation.'

'Does Mr. Hunter know the trouble he's caused?' Evelyn asked the Feingolds.

Mr. Feingold nodded. 'He does. He hopes to one day make amends, but until then, he will reside in London.'

'Sabastien really does hope that time will help heal any selfish wrongdoings,' Miss Feingold added.

'Time may heal some of the trouble he caused,' said Mr. Ashby. 'But when the feelings of young ladies are hurt, they may never be completely restored to their full admiration.' He referred to the inadvertent distress caused to Charmaine. Everyone knew what he meant.

'That is why I want the truth and the mistakes spoken honestly,' Mr. Feingold told them. 'I want nothing hidden, so if you have anything to ask me, do so now.'

'What are your intentions regarding Charmaine?' Mr. Midwinter asked him outright.

Mr. Feingold's reply was equally clear. 'I wish to ask her to marry me.'

His words were so unexpected that they caused the others to pause.

Mr. Feingold continued on the back of their stunned silence. 'I want us to become engaged this summer. And when we're married, I'd like Charmaine to live with me at Heather Park.' He looked at Charmaine, knowing he was risking everything by expressing his love for her so clearly.

But the sincerity of his reply, although it hit them with unexpected shock, restored their faith in Mr. Feingold's fine character. They began to realise that it was in anger that he'd left, and most of them secretly knew they'd act in a similar way if they'd been put in that position by Mr. Hunter.

Crispin Midwinter glanced at Charmaine. She stood beside him, her face pale from the shock of seeing Rupert at the ball, and then receiving his proposal in front of everyone.

'Are you all right?' Mr. Midwinter asked her.

Charmaine hesitated before replying. 'Yes, no...but I feel I shall be fine.' She looked at Rupert, seeing the sorrow in his expression that he'd hurt her and now wanted her forgiveness. In her heart, she knew she would forgive him, for she loved him dearly. Seeing him again brought back floods of emotions, and all of them led to one wonderful realisation. She would accept Rupert's proposal. She would become engaged to him this summer. And she would love to live with him at Heather Park, for she could still be near Crispin and the Ashby family.

'I would also like to state my intentions,' Captain DeGrey announced. While everyone that mattered to him was present, there was no better time to speak up. Hesitation cost him in the past. No hesitation tonight.

They all looked at the captain, especially Evelyn. She was both hopeful and hesitant, wondering what he was going to say.

'It is my dearest wish to ask Evelyn to marry me. To become engaged this summer. For Evelyn to be my wife and live with me at Seaforth.'

Mr. Ashby smiled as his wife clutched his arm to steady herself. The news was wonderful, but so unexpected. She was quite overcome.

But Mr. Ashby bore the surprise with broad shoulders and a warm feeling in his heart. His dear Evelyn he knew would be happy with the captain. He'd sensed for some time that there was a deep connection between them. Getting to know Captain DeGrey from their friendly encounters, he found himself liking the captain. He believed he would take great care of his daughter, and that Evelyn would be happy.

Mr. Ashby smiled and announced cheerfully without expecting a response to his remark. 'If there are any other gentlemen planning to marry the young ladies of our acquaintance, please speak up now.'

Crispin Midwinter decided to take a chance and spoke up. 'As we're all declaring our devotion, I wish to tell you it is my intention to become engaged to Annabel Ashby. To marry her and have her live as my wife at Blackhall.'

Annabel looked stunned. She blinked in disbelief that Mr. Midwinter would be so bold. But after the surprise, she started to smile and then they all laughed lightly.

Mr. Ashby clapped his hands with glee. 'I knew there was true affection between you and my Annabel.'

'This is wonderful news,' Mrs. Ashby trilled. 'Two daughters to be married, and Charmaine too. What a romantic and delightful summer we'll all have.'

Mr. Ashby put his arm around Mrs. Ashby's shoulder and they stood together smiling at their daughters.

Primrose was pleased for her sisters, and bore no hint of envy. She knew her time for romance was coming. She'd already danced with two fine gentlemen at the ball and she was delighted that Evelyn and Annabel were to marry for love.

Raine Feingold stood beside Rupert as he smiled at both her and Charmaine. There was no handsome gentleman to offer her his hand in marriage, but she believed that happy events encouraged more happy events and that the man for her would one day walk into her life. She was delighted to be living again at Heather Park. This in itself made her smile. The short visit to London confirmed one thing in particular. She didn't miss London and preferred staying at Heather Park.

The excitement of the evening continued with the new couples taking to the dance floor, along with Mr. and Mrs. Ashby. Raine Feingold and Primrose soon found themselves dancing again with fine gentlemen.

As Captain DeGrey and Evelyn danced together, he took a few moments to dance her over to a doorway that led outside into the front garden. Taking her hand, he hurried out and they stood breathless from exhilaration, from the dancing and their new engagement, looking at the view. The sea sparkled like liquid silver and the warm summer air was filled with the scent of flowers in the garden that included night scented stock.

They were still in view of the couples dancing, but he wanted a moment to express his feelings to Evelyn. He faced her, gazing down into her beautiful face and held her hands in his.

'I have hoped for so long for this moment,' he began. 'I love you, Evelyn. I've always loved you, and I always will.'

'I love you too,' she said softly.

He leaned down and kissed her, sealing their promise to marry.

She felt his firm lips were filled with longing and love for her.

'I must tell you,' he said quickly, 'that it is my intension for us to be the first couple to be married. I will not hesitate, not this time.'

Evelyn smiled and nodded, and her heart could barely contain her excitement.

'Come on, Domenic!' a voice called out to him from the dance floor.

They looked round to see Crispin Midwinter, partnered with Annabel, waving urgently to them.

'Hurry up!' said Mr. Midwinter. 'We can't let Mr. Ashby and that scoundrel Rupert Feingold beat us in the dancing. They're already threatening to challenge us to a game of cards later. And we all know how that will end.'

The captain and Evelyn laughed and hurried inside to rejoin the company. Rupert smiled at them while he danced with Charmaine, and Mr. Ashby had a mischievous grin as he danced with his wife.

The musicians played another popular song and the dancing became ever more lively. Laughter, love and merriment created a party atmosphere in the ballroom, and the happy couples and their friends danced well into the night. It was a night that would linger long in all their memories, but there were plenty of other evenings of fun and friendship in their futures together.

Evelyn gazed at the captain as they danced, knowing in her heart that she had made the right choice to marry this wonderful man.

End

Heather Park Regency Romance Embroidery Patterns

Embroidery was one of the themes of Heather Park Regency Romance. Embroidery patterns designed by the author, De-ann Black, are available free from the book's accompanying website. These include: bluebells, forget-me-nots, daisies, pansies, heather, night scented stock, dragonfly, butterflies and bees.

The patterns shown here in the book are not to scale.

Colour pictures of the embroidery are shown on the book's website.

You can download the full size patterns here:
De-annBlack.com/Regency

Bluebells and Butterflies

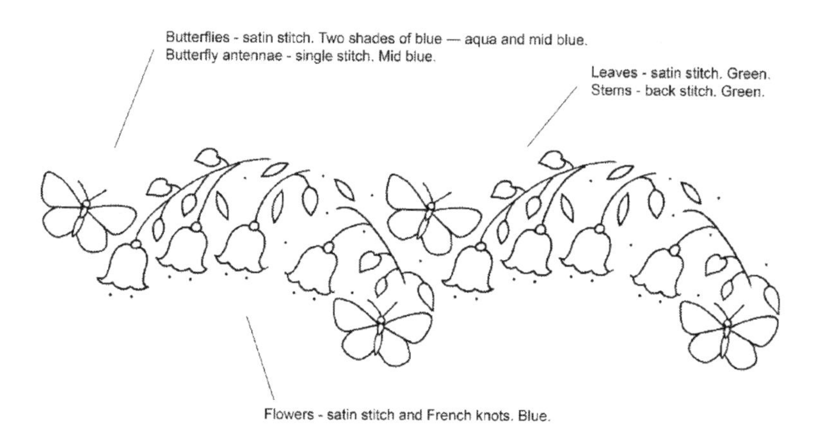

Satin stitch the bluebell flowers in blue.
Add blue French knots (or single small stitches).
Back stitch the stems in green.
Stitch the leaves using satin stitch in green.
Add green French knots (or a single small stitch).
Use two shades of blue (aqua and mid blue) to satin stitch the butterflies.
Add single stitches in mid blue for the antennae.

Thread

Use two strands of embroidery floss, or 1 strand of 12wt cotton thread for all of these embroidery patterns.

Forget-me-nots

Forget-me-nots

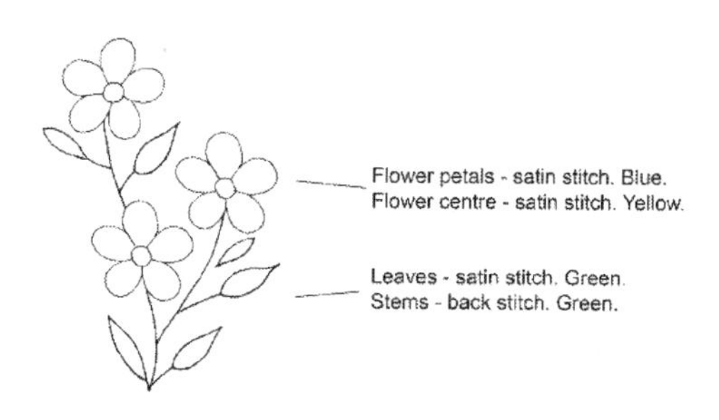

Satin stitch the petals with blue.
Satin stitch the centre with yellow.
Stitch the leaves using satin stitch in green.
Back stitch the stems with green.

Thread

Use two strands of embroidery floss, or 1 strand of 12wt cotton thread for all of these embroidery patterns.

Pansy

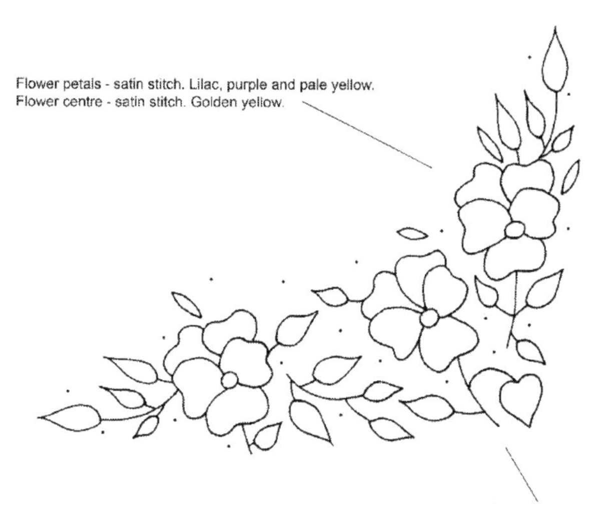

Satin stitch the petals with lilac, purple and pale yellow.
Satin stitch the centre with golden yellow.
Stitch the leaves using satin stitch in green.
Back stitch the stems in green.
Add green French knots (or a single small stitch).

Thread

Use two strands of embroidery floss, or 1 strand of 12wt cotton thread for all of these embroidery patterns.

Daisy and Queen Anne's Lace

Flower petals - satin stitch. White.
Flower centre - satin stitch. Yellow.

French knots. White.

Leaves - satin stitch & single stitch. Green.
Stems - stem stitch. Green.

Satin stitch the petals with white.
Satin stitch the centre with golden yellow.
Stitch the leaves using satin stitch and single stitch in green.
Stem stitch the stems in green.
Add white French knots (or a single small stitch).

Thread

Use two strands of embroidery floss, or 1 strand of 12wt cotton thread for all of these embroidery patterns.

Heather

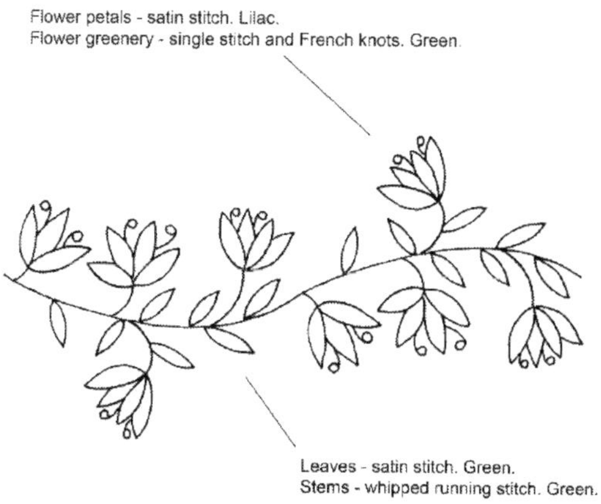

Flower petals - satin stitch. Lilac.
Flower greenery - single stitch and French knots. Green.

Leaves - satin stitch. Green.
Stems - whipped running stitch. Green.

Satin stitch the petals in lilac.
Single stitch the greenery in green. Add green French knots (or single small stitches).
Stitch the leaves using satin stitch in green.
Use a whipped running stitch to embroider the stems in green.

Thread

Use two strands of embroidery floss, or 1 strand of 12wt cotton thread for all of these embroidery patterns.

Night Scented Stock

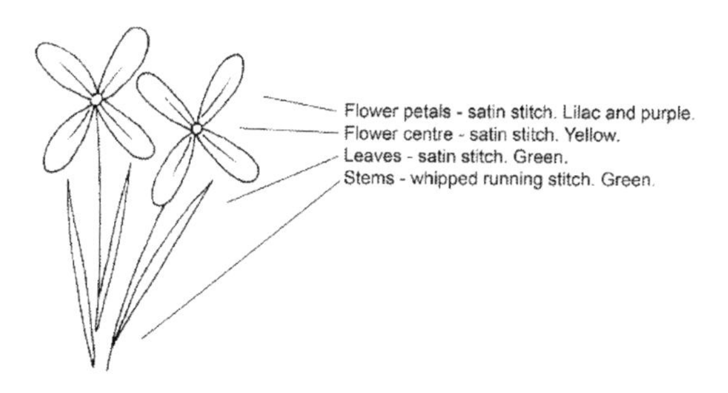

Satin stitch the petals with lilac, and highlight with a single purple stitch.
Satin stitch the centre with yellow.
Stitch the leaves using satin stitch with green.
Use a whipped running stitch to embroider the stems with green.

Thread

Use two strands of embroidery floss, or 1 strand of 12wt cotton thread for all of these embroidery patterns.

Butterflies, Bees and Dragonflies

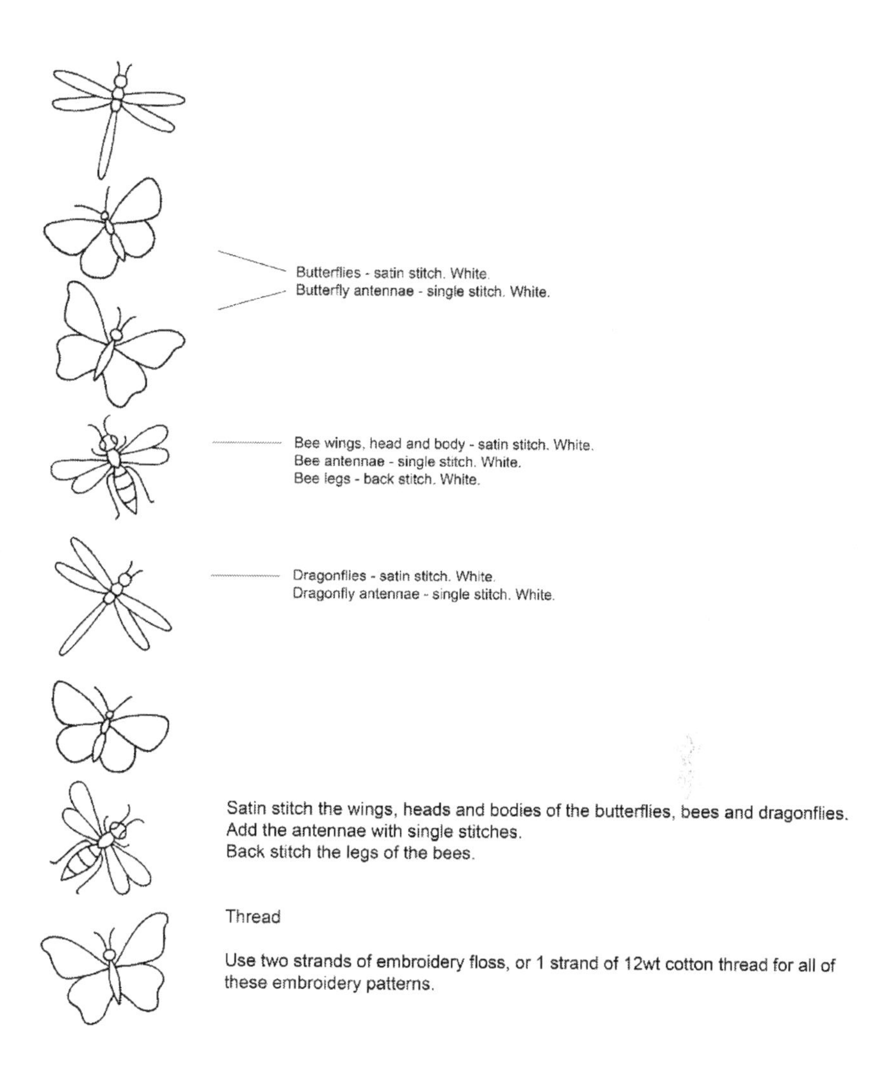

Satin stitch the wings, heads and bodies of the butterflies, bees and dragonflies.
Add the antennae with single stitches.
Back stitch the legs of the bees.

Thread

Use two strands of embroidery floss, or 1 strand of 12wt cotton thread for all of these embroidery patterns.

About the Author:

De-ann Black is a bestselling author, scriptwriter and former newspaper journalist. She has over 70 books published. Romance, crime thrillers, espionage novels, action adventure. And children's books (non-fiction rocket science books and children's fiction). She became an Amazon All-Star author in 2014 and 2015.

She previously worked as a full-time newspaper journalist for several years. She had her own weekly columns in the press. This included being a motoring correspondent where she got to test drive cars every week for the press for three years.

Before being asked to work for the press, De-ann worked in magazine editorial writing everything from fashion features to social news. She was the marketing editor of a glossy magazine. She is also a professional artist and illustrator. Fabric design, dressmaking, sewing, knitting and fashion are part of her work.

Additionally, De-ann has always been interested in fitness, and was a fitness and bodybuilding champion, 100 metre runner and mountaineer. As a former N.A.B.B.A. Miss Scotland, she had a weekly fitness show on the radio that ran for over three years.

De-ann trained in Shukokai karate, boxing, kickboxing, Dayan Qigong and Jiu Jitsu. She is currently based in Scotland.

Her colouring books and embroidery design books are available in paperback. These include Floral Nature Embroidery Designs and Scottish Garden Embroidery Designs.

Find out more at: www.de-annblack.com

Printed in Great Britain
by Amazon